Mills & Boon
Best Seller Romance

A chance to read and collect some of the best-loved novels from Mills & Boon – the world's largest publisher of romantic fiction.

Every month, four titles by favourite Mills & Boon authors will be re-published in the *Best Seller Romance* series.

A list of other titles in the *Best Seller Romance* series can be found at the end of this book.

Violet Winspear

FORBIDDEN RAPTURE

MILLS & BOON LIMITED
LONDON · TORONTO

First published 1973
Australian copyright 1981
Philippine copyright 1981
This edition 1981

ISBN 0 263 73626 1

Set in Linotype Baskerville 10 on 11 pt.

Made and printed in Great Britain by Richard Clay (The Chaucer Press) Ltd, Bungay, Suffolk

CHAPTER ONE

The slim, fair girl came aboard alone, a mink coat draped around her shoulders with orchids on the lapel. When she reached the head of the gangway she gave her name and cabin number to the young officer on duty there, and the ready smile which he had been giving to other passengers was absent from his face as he stared a moment at Della Neve. Then a shy look came into his eyes.

'It's a pleasure to have you aboard, Miss Neve.' He gave her a smart salute. 'I once heard you sing in *La Bohème* at the Metropolitan and it was a memorable experience.'

'Thank you.' Her speaking voice had an attractive huskiness, and her smile lingered only a moment before it was gone. 'The *Gothic Star* seems a nice ship and I'm sure I'm going to enjoy the cruise.'

'I hope, Miss Neve, that you will sing for us one evening?'

'I'm afraid that won't be possible.' She gazed straight at him with blue-green eyes like frozen gems, then she handed him her passport and tickets and followed a steward to her state cabin, while another followed with her handcases. They went along a wide central companionway to the main deck and along a corridor whose carpet was a deep blue colour. A door was opened for her and she entered the suite which would be hers for the next six weeks, while the *Gothic Star* cruised the blue waters of the Mediterranean.

Left alone in the solitary luxury of her state cabin, Della removed her mink coat and let it fall carelessly to a white velvet couch, where it draped itself like a dark-furred animal, while the orchids lay crushed beneath its weight. She wandered a moment to the porthole and could hear music drifting from the tannoy; a sentimental waltz tune which reminded her of Vienna and that wonderful evening when she had sung in the courtyard of the Ravenholtz Castle. Marsh had thought it marvellous as well, for the very next day he had taken her for a drive through the Vienna woods and there . . .

She sighed and glanced at her left hand. On the wrist of that hand was a slim, gleaming jade bracelet, and on the third finger was a gold ring set with a matching, priceless jade.

There had been no way to refuse Marsh; her heart had not been proof against the diffident, almost boyish smile on his face when he had taken her hand, kissed it, and slipped on to her finger the ring set with a jade to match the bracelet he had given her on her twenty-second birthday. As in everything he had not questioned or truly asked, for it was not in the character of such a man of business to let an opportunity slip by. It was often said that he had a golden flair for picking the right moment, and there in the autumn-gold woods, in possibly the most romantic city in the world, he had chosen his moment well, and Della had drifted into their engagement as the evening before she had drifted into a waltz with him.

Though he was often referred to as 'face of stone' by his business rivals and his many employees, Della alone knew the reverse side of the million-dollar coin. She owed everything to Marsh Graham; her life and her education: her career and this cruise.

This blue-water cruise which was meant to unlock the band of nerves which had taken possession of her throat, so that singing a mere *chanson* was a torment, and the singing of an aria an impossibility. Marsh, ever concerned for her, had rushed her off in his Blue-Cloud Rolls to see his specialist in Harley Street. 'Nerves!' Sheer nerves and the natural, accumulative anxieties of the star performer.

A star, in fact, who had risen in the firmament of opera with a brilliant, breathtaking speed, accelerated by the will and fortune of her guardian, the formidable Marsh Graham who on a wet and stormy evening, when she was only ten years old, had pulled her from the wreckage of her parents' car and taken charge of her life from that time onwards.

Discovering that she had an ear for music and a sweet voice, he had set about at once having her trained in all the arts of being a real singer. She had been taught to know about Bach and Wagner before she was twelve years old. By the time she was seventeen she was in the hands of one of the best Italian teachers of singing in the world, a true maestro who had firmly told Marsh that she would sing like an angel in the Italian operas, but since she was not built on the lines of Kundry and Brünnhilde, he must not expect her to bring down the roof. Her voice was angelic, her face was lovely and she would make a divine Mimi, and a touching Madame Butterfly.

Marsh, ever shrewd and authoritative, had arranged for her debut on the eve of her nineteenth birthday, when in his opinion she was a rose in the bud and would be the most appealing Mimi to appear on the opera stage for years. Again he had picked his golden moment, and Della had sung in the arms of Rodolfo with all the lilting, innocent pleading of a girl desiring love and being fearful of it at the same time.

Perhaps she alone knew that her interpretation of the role sprang from her own inward awareness that Marsh planned to be her demanding and possessive lover.

Now, as the engines of the *Gothic Star* began to beat like a great heart, and the music changed to *Beyond the Blue Horizon*, Della did something that was unplanned and wholly instinctive . . . she tore from her finger the ring which Marsh had put there and glanced round wildly for some place to hide it. On the vanity table stood a tall vase of exquisite white roses, and knowing Marsh had sent these to the ship, as he had sent the big circular box of Austrian chocolates and the small pile of the very latest novels, she winced at her own act of betrayal, but she could not return the ring to her finger, and snatching up her handbag she swiftly opened it and dropped the ring inside, out of sight.

Later on, when she was feeling calmer, she would replace the ring and resume her sense of belonging, body and soul, to Marsh. For twelve years she had been his 'property', for he was intensely aware of what he owned and directed, but for six weeks, cut off from him by the blue water, she would be her own person.

She snapped shut her bag and before leaving her cabin to walk for a while on deck she touched a finger to the white roses. Always white, flooding her dressing-room when she sang, scenting her bedroom at Cascades, the house which Marsh owned at Richmond, named not for a waterfall, he said, but for the cascades of notes which her warm soprano voice could produce.

Her fingers clenched about the roses, and then she winced again as a thorn stabbed her finger and left a drop of blood on a white bud. Snatching up her mink coat, for it would be cool on deck until the ship steamed into warmer waters, she flung it around her shoulders and left her cabin, not forgetting to lock the door behind her. Everything she owned had been given her by Marsh, therefore she owned a lot of pretty but expensive things. She followed the long sweep of blue carpet to a flight of steps leading up to the promenade deck. The evocative music was still playing, and now all visitors had gone ashore and were waving from the wharfside, while passengers leaned from the rails of the ship and waved back, calling good-bye.

'Bon voyage!' The voices blended below to carry the words. *'Bon voyage!'*

Della stood by the rails gazing downwards at the upturned faces and the waving handkerchiefs, while here and there on the deck a handkerchief was pressed to a woman's eyes as the ship moved away from the wharf in a swirl of muddy green water, while the tugs hooted and heaved and guided the great ship on the start of her voyage. The music faded away and there was a silence filled with the crying of sea-birds as the wharf and the customs shed and the fluttering flags grew smaller and smaller.

There had been no one to see Della off on her voyage, for Marsh had left London on business two days ago, and as she stood alone on the deck she felt an aching amazement at her own sense of relief. She felt almost like a truant child who had escaped for a while a too watchful parent.

Her left hand, freed of his ring, gripped the rail and her heart seemed to beat in unison with the deep pulsing of the ship's engines. The long trail of foamy bubbles that the ship was whipping up with the propellers seemed to be expressive of the excitement that was starting to bubble in her veins.

Marsh was generous and protective, but – Della flung back her head in a gesture of freedom and welcomed the coolness of the wind through her hair – but she had begun to feel as smothered as a gem in a velvet box. For years she had been cushioned against the buffs of life, ever since that awful night when she had lost both mother and father and the tall stranger with the silver-gilt hair had swept her up in his arms and cared for her ever since.

With all her heart she was grateful to Marsh, but she couldn't help but wonder what it felt like to feel the wild and glorious abandon of Mimi, or the sensuous surrender of Butterfly. Deep in her heart she hungered for romance; she longed to feel wholly alive and not merely the cosseted singing ward of a very rich man. She wanted the excitement, the peril, the aching joy of being romanced and not owned – owned by a man to whom she owed everything, the silk on her body, the shine on her hair, the polish on her speech. Her real name had been Dolly Neve, but Marsh had changed that to the glamour of Della. Her father had been a car-assembly worker, taking his wife and child to the seaside for a holiday. Her home had been in the suburbs of London, and from out of a leggy scrap of a schoolgirl Marsh had fashioned a lovely, slim, talented creature who wore her expensive clothes with *élan* and who could read a music score at a glance and speak four langages. He had moulded her as if she were Galatea, and she knew with what gallantry and patience he had waited to claim his reward.

At the finale of this cruise she and Marsh were to be married, and nothing on earth would stop her from marrying him – but right now, right this moment she was free and afloat on the ocean, with no ring on her finger, and no personal maid to watch her every movement. She had left Rose at the house, against the orders of Marsh, and that was why today her fair hair was free about her face instead of beautifully coiffured to suggest a more sophisticated Della Neve than the one she looked at this precise moment.

Despite the rich darkness of her mink coat there was a certain youth and loneliness about her, and sensing this in herself she turned from the ship's rail to survey the promenade deck and those travellers who still lingered, as she did, though the wharf was now lost to sight and that trail of foam was already a few miles long.

The *Gothic Star* had cast her lines, and the wide, hungry, unpredictable waters were pulling her into a powerful embrace. She had surrendered to the sea, and her heart, deep down inside the graceful body of steel, thumped with powerful energy.

In that moment, as excitement coursed through Della

and lit her blue-green eyes, she became aware that she and one other person shared this rather solitary end of the deck and with the heightened curiosity which being at sea brings to a traveller she took a glance at the man . . . he stood by the ship's rail, tall and dark in a perfectly tailored suit, quietly smoking a cigar with a self-contained ease and enjoyment. Della had meant to look away after satisfying her curiosity, but there was something about that dark, arresting silhouette against the deepening dusk of the sky that held her attention, and held it beyond that moment when she could have withdrawn her gaze and not been caught staring at him.

Too late . . . he suddenly turned his head in her direction and their glances interlocked and the shock of it went through Della like a knife. There was an ageless, almost pagan beauty about the set of his head, and the strong slanting cheekbones. The darkness of his hair was matched by his eyes, and there was a cleft in the centre of his firm, dark chin. Every detail of the man was arresting, from the perfect fit of his grey-blue suit down to his hand-crafted shoes, but what gripped and held Della was the scar on his left cheekbone, for it had the exact shape of a diamond, branded there in the olive darkness of his skin.

Abruptly she was confused and she turned away from him before he could see the colour that stormed into her cheeks. She hastened along the deck to the stairs, and the strangest thing of all was that her knees were trembling and she felt the exact sensation of fright that she had felt on her first appearance on the stage. Her heart was thumping and her skin was hot and cold at the same time.

'*Signorina*.'

The word arrested her and she had glanced round before she could stop herself. His long stride had brought him almost at her heels and she had a sensation of being towered over. She stopped walking, as if instinct warned her that he would reach out and stop her. 'Yes, what is it?' she asked, and once again her blue-green eyes were fixed upon that diamond-shaped scar that somehow set the seal on his striking difference from other men she had seen.

'Your orchids.' He held them out to her, with an air of a suave politeness. She glanced swiftly at her lapel and saw that they had become unpinned and had dropped from her coat to the deck.

'Oh – thank you.' She took them with her left hand, for she was holding her bag with the other hand, and she was aware that his eyes skimmed her fingers and she thought guiltily of the ring that she had thrust into her bag, out of sight but not out of mind.

'So I was right to address you as *signorina*.' His voice was deep, with many subtle shadings to it. It was also cultured, with just enough of an accent to increase its resonant appeal. 'We appear, you and I, to be solitary travellers, or have you a family down below in a cabin?'

Della almost caught her breath aloud, for she knew that in the suavest way possible she was being 'picked up' and there was no Marsh, hovering tall and stern, to protect her from this Italian stranger whose face played such odd tricks with her usual good sense. What should she do? Rake out her engagement ring and put it on, or invent a whole parcel of relatives?

Then, as she hesitated in her reply, he inclined his head and his heels came together in a whisper of a click. 'Let me introduce myself, *signorina*. I am Nicholas Franquila, and I prefer to be called Nick by those I am hopeful of knowing a little better. Perhaps you would join me in the bar for a glass of champagne and a sandwich? To stay the pangs of hunger until dinner, eh?'

'No – thank you.' Della made her eyes look cool and

disinterested, for he was obviously a Latin wolf who sensed that she *was* all alone and therefore vulnerable. 'I have to see the Purser, and then I have some unpacking to do. Good-bye—'

'It can hardly be good-bye on a ship,' he broke in, sardonically. 'Fate may see to it that I sit next to you at dinner; who can tell, when Fate is also female and therefore unpredictable.'

'I assure you, *signore*, that I am very predictable.' Della spoke in her coolest voice, and she looked at him with all the hauteur of the young *diva*. 'I never drink champagne with a stranger, nor do I play any of the usual cosmopolitan games of chance. I don't doubt that you are an expert, and at the moment you are all alone in need of a satellite and I chanced to come into your orbit. But this ship is a fairly large one and I'm sure you will shortly find much more dazzling company than I—'

'But you are a star, Miss Neve, and what could be more dazzling than that?'

Della stared at him. 'So you knew all along who I was?'

'Not right away,' he corrected her. 'On stage you appear to be more self-assured, and your hair is always more soigné. You suit your name – Lady of Snow.'

'And you suit yours,' she flashed back at him. 'Nick the Devil!'

Never ... never had Della been so impertinent to anyone, and he seemed to make things worse by laughing softly and deeply in his throat and looking at her with a dark sort of threat in his eyes. She turned hastily away from him and ran down the stairs to the main deck, and still with a sense of flight she found her stateroom and unlocked the door with a hand that trembled slightly. Oh, this was ridiculous! She felt highly annoyed with herself for allowing that Latin wolf to ruffle her composure in this silly way. It was what he had set out to do, and she, forgetful of all she had learned from Marsh, had fallen into his suave and mocking trap.

Making an effort to forget the dark and arresting face of the man, she unlocked her pigskin cases and her trunk and began to hang her dresses, for day and evening wear, in the capacious closet, with a shelf for shoes and another for scarves and other accessories. She placed all her diaphanous lingerie in the chest of drawers, and then stood gazing at her jewel-case for several moments before unlocking it. There in the tiny drawers all velvet-lined lay the various lovely presents from Marsh. The set of turquoise jewellery, the pearls and the sapphire cross, the brooches that sparkled with all the soft lustre of real worth, and the matching diamond bracelets. She drew a little sigh, and with a curious effort she imposed the face of her fiancé upon that of the patrician yet slightly wicked face of the man she had so recently encountered on the promenade deck.

Marsh could not be called handsome, but he was distinguished, with one of those slightly tired and clever faces, aged before its time by the many responsibilities of the successful business man. Gradually over the years Della had seen his gilt hair become more and more silver, and this added to his distinction. And he always dressed in the dark greys and blues of the English tycoon. He was repected and a little feared wherever he went, and his only real form of relaxation was the opera. Marsh knew almost everything there was to know about superb music, yet he couldn't play a note on any instrument, nor could he sing in key.

Della smiled a little and fingered the tiny jewelled fan which Marsh had given her after she had sung in that operatic adaptation of *Lady Windermere's Fan* by the composer everyone referred to as Cavaltivani. It was well known that this was a pseudonym, and even in musical circles no one had been successful in tracking down the owner of the invented name. But everyone agreed that he had a remarkable talent, and opera producers and singers alike awaited with eagerness the next piece of work from his lyrical pen.

This collection of jewellery, given by Marsh with a courtly kindness which had never really concealed his sense of ownership towards her, was too valuable to be left in her stateroom, but Della didn't relock the case before adding her jade bracelet and her engagement ring. She had some costume jewellery which could be worn in the evenings, and she still had this strong, almost desperate desire to belong only to herself while she was a passenger aboard the *Gothic Star*.

Very firmly she locked the jewel-case and took all the precious contents to the Purser. She returned to her quarters feeling a sense of lightness and release. She also felt a stab of hunger and rang for the steward to bring her some coffee and sandwiches. 'It'll be a pleasure, Miss Neve.' He gave her a broad smile. 'My missus dotes on them *chansons* you recorded a few months ago. Real love songs, she calls them, and a bit of a change from all that pop screaming. What sandwiches would you like, miss? There's some lovely cold beef, or you could have grouse. A gentleman ordered some a while ago—'

'Beef, please.' She returned his smile. 'What's your name, steward? I'd like us to be friends.'

'It's Larkin, miss, and my missus will be downright delighted when I write to let her know that I'm looking after the famous Della Neve. I hope you'll soon be making some more of those romantic records?'

'I – I don't know, Larkin.' Della clasped her throat with her hand and felt again the shock and bewilderment of not being able to break into warm, clear song. 'I'm resting my voice at the present time and I just want to relax on this cruise and not think about work – is it a good trip? I do hope so.'

'A very nice one, miss, as soon as we hit the warm waters. We call at some interesting ports and it's always fun to go ashore. It's a shame you're travelling all alone, but you'll soon pick up with a – with a pal.' He grinned and hurried away to fetch her beef sandwiches and coffee, and these were waiting for her on a covered tray when she came from her shower, wearing a short towelling jacket that revealed her long slim legs, and with her fair hair damp and curling at the edges, She sat on a little velvet chair and ate her snack; the beef was delicious, and the coffee brown and sweet. So far Della was untroubled by the weight problems of some of the other singers she had performed with, and Marsh had ensured that she followed a routine of tennis and swimming that kept her trim and fit.

She picked up a magazine and flipped through it ... and then she stared and gripped the glossy pages as her gaze met the dark, lazily worldly eyes of one of the persons featured in the magazine. The man was photographed standing beside the American heiress Sorine Hunter, and the columnist hinted that the beautiful Sorine, twice married before, was thinking of adding to her collection the Conte Nicholas di Fioro Franquila, the Continental heart-throb who was reputed to have a certain air of mystery about him, but who was definitely known to have had his name linked with several other ladies of good fortune and good looks. 'Had he now been hunted down and finally captured?' the columnist coyly asked of her readers.

Della wasn't impressed by his title, but she was definitely confirmed in her opinion that he was an experienced pursuer of the ladies; the sort who cashed in on his looks and his background and led a totally useless life chasing after heiresses and getting his face featured in the glossies. She felt that such men were contemptible and she vowed to herself that she would give him the icy brush-off if he dared to speak to her again.

For the next hour she rested on the *chaise-longue,* with the ends of her hair in the large rollers that would give a soft undercurl to her hair which was thick and aspen-gold. Without Rose to attend to those soigné styles she would on this trip wear her hair in the simple ways that really appealed to her. She rested her head on a little silk pillow and closed her eyes, and though she couldn't feel the motion of the ship she had a sensation of floating away from all her cares, and from her guilty relief that Marsh had been too busy to travel with her on the *Gothic Star.*

She slept for an hour and and awoke feeling wonderfully refreshed. This being the first night at sea, the passengers were excused from being too formal and she chose to wear a short, full-skirted dress in dusty-pink cashmere. It was cut on the simple, perfect lines of the couture garment, and her sleek dark-honey nylons and high-heeled court shoes showed off to advantage her long and graceful legs. She might have been a dancer rather than a singer, and because she was a singer and trained in counterpoint and rhythm, she walked with the grace of a girl with music in her veins.

The restaurant deck was below the main deck, and Della paused at the glass doors before entering. Already quite a few people were seated at their tables, and she noticed the attractive decor of the dining-room, with glass panels etched with birds and flowers filtering a romantic light down on to the tables. As she stood hesitant a waiter came to her side and inquired her name. He then led her to a table for four persons. Two of them were already there, and they glanced up briefly from the blue and silver menus to give her a welcoming smile; a young couple who had a look of honeymoon about them. She smiled in return and sat down to study her own menu. Turtle soup to start with, she decided, the canvasback duck with fresh peas and small potatoes, followed by a vanilla mousse.

Her decision made, she sat back to take a discreet look around the room. Some of the male diners were gazing at her with admiring interest, and quite a few of the women were assessing her looks, the cut and cost of her dress, and the possible value of the coral necklace she was wearing. She wasn't certain she was recognized as Della Neve until the orchestra on its half-concealed dais began to play *We'll Gather Lilacs*, the lovely Ivor Novello song which she had recorded several months ago and whose sales had soared into the best-selling charts.

The music had almost reached its finale when a slight buzzing broke out at nearby tables and Della saw that the doors had opened to admit a tall figure in a dark and perfect lounge suit. At once the head waiter was at his elbow, and then to her horror Della saw that the Conte Nicholas de Fioro Franquila was being conducted straight towards the table she occupied with the young couple, who were discreetly holding hands under cover of the lace cloth.

The Conte's dark eyes were looking directly at Della, and they were mocking her shocked expression.

'Fate,' she seemed to read in those Italian eyes, 'is the most unpredictable of females.'

Della was tensed in every nerve as he came closer still to their table, and then with a suave indifference passed right by in the wake of the *maître d'hôtel* and headed in the direction of a six-person table, where the Captain rose to greet the Conte, and where a striking woman in a coffee-coloured dress, patterned with panels of beads, gave him a look that could only be called inviting.

As he sat down at the Captain's table, a man slipped into the seat beside Della and shook out his table napkin. The action caught her eye and she looked at him.

He was ordinary and friendly, and his accent was a

northern one as he calmly introduced himself. 'How do, folks. My name is Joe Hartley and I'm in the grocery business.' He gave a grin. 'Super grocery they call it these days, and now let's see what they're giving us for dinner our first night out.'

Della was later to learn that Joe had recently lost his beloved wife and was taking this cruise in order to get over his grief. But right now he was a sociable barrier, his large frame blocking out that nearby table and the sixth occupant of it. She had felt certain that he had been heading for the chair beside her own, and it was mortifying that she had not shown a total indifference at his approach. Now he had the satisfaction of knowing that he had panicked her again, and as she remembered the mocking glint in his eyes, her cheeks burned and it was a relief when the waiter brought her turtle soup and she could concentrate on her dinner.

The honeymoon couple murmured to each other throughout the meal, but Joe Hartley was a sociable soul and he kept up a steady stream of talk, mostly about food and the rising prices of everything, but as soon as she could escape gracefully from the restaurant Della did so, and breathing deeply the cool night air she made her way up the double flight of stairs to the lounge deck, all but deserted and lit here and there by wall lights which cast small pools of illumination among the friendly shadows.

Della walked there alone for a while, and then when she heard a double set of footsteps and heard a woman laugh seductively, she swiftly concealed herself in the shadows, barely breathing as a man and a woman strolled by and Havana cigar smoke mingled with a breath of elegant perfume in the folds of a coffee-coloured dress whose panels of beads sparkled softly.

'You are a devil, Count Nicholas,' the woman scolded. 'You know full well everyone has you half-way to the altar with the Divine Hunter, so don't you dare deny it.'

'I would not dream of denying you a thing, *signora,*' he drawled, and there in the shadows Della held her evening purse against her heart, as if the small object might offer protection against the alarming magnetism of his voice. The couple passed out of earshot, but fearful that they might retrace their steps in this direction, Della slipped into the cinema lounge and found a seat in the dim, scented haven.

Count Nicholas, the woman had called him, not Nick ... Nick the Devil!

CHAPTER TWO

SUNLIGHT streamed through the portholes and struck across the silk coverlet which had been pushed restlessly to the carpet. Gradually the sunlight increased in brightness until all at once it was caressing the eyelids of the occupant of the bed. They flickered as they felt the warmth and suddenly they fluttered open and blue-green eyes were gazing with bewilderment at the circular windows.

Sunshine ... a scent of the ocean stealing in through the half-open portholes ... Della smiled and sat up stretching her arms. The ship must now be miles from England and sailing into the blue waters leading to the island of Zattere, their first port of call.

Swiftly she was out of bed and on her way to look from the nearest porthole at the blue water. She caught her breath in delight, and she knew that Marsh would have been amazed by her youthful, almost naïve appreciation of the silky ocean met by the clear sunlit sky, for this was not the first time she had travelled on a ship. A couple of times they had crossed the Atlantic on one of the big liners, when she had been booked to sing at the Metropolitan, but never before had she been entirely on her own.

She turned to look around her stateroom and was savouring her sense of freedom when she noticed the bed coverlet on the floor, an indication that she had slept restlessly. She picked it up and told herself that it was perfectly natural for someone to toss and turn their first night of a sea trip all alone.

A glanced at her small clock informed her that she had an hour to spare before it was time for breakfast, which she had chosen to have in the restaurant instead of her stateroom. Well, she would shower and dress, and then write a letter to Marsh. It couldn't be posted until they arrived at Zattere, but writing it would help pass the time. She glanced at her left hand, which had such a bare look after being adorned by the jade ring for the past few months. As she wandered into the bathroom and turned on the shower, she guiltily wondered if she ought to go to the Purser later on and resume wearing her engagement ring. She let her nightdress slip to the floor and covered her hair with a bath-cap, slim and white as she stepped under the water. It seemed so disloyal to Marsh to remove the ring and have it locked away, as if she didn't truly love him. But of course she loved him! She couldn't imagine life without Marsh to turn to when she was in need of advice and friendship ...

Della bit her lip and turned the shower full on, so the water bounced against her skin and provided some protection against her traumatic thoughts.

Was that all marriage with Marsh meant to her ... a protective friendship, a guiding hand, a continuance of the security he had always provided for her?

She turned off the shower and as the steam cleared from the wall mirror she gazed at her wet reflected body and saw the droplets of water sliding down over her white limbs, her slim shoulders, and small pert breasts. Why was it that her body felt no thrill of any sort when she contemplated with Marsh all the ultimate intimacies of marriage? Why didn't those shudders of ecstasy rake her when he took her in his arms and kissed her? She knew she cared for him, and so her cool response to his ardour could only mean that she was like her name ... made of snow.

Out of a cloud of talcum which matched her skin perfume she slipped into her lingerie, a pale turquoise colour to tone with the turquoise tunic-suit which she decided to wear. She combed her hair and looped it in a barrette of pale gold at the nape of her neck, and because she liked to keep her skin free of make-up when she was not singing in the heavy make-up of opera night after night, she merely applied a light touch of pink to her lips and was ready to face the day ahead of her.

It was now eight-thirty and deciding that her letter to Marsh could wait a while she left her cabin and went up on to the promenade deck for a walk before breakfast. Several people were doing the same and they gave her a cheery greeting as they passed by. 'Excellent morning, eh? If this kind of weather keeps up we'll have a real sunshine cruise. Look at that sea! Like liquid silk!'

It was, indeed. A rich, glittering, living sheet of silk, making a silken rustling sound as the waves slapped against the sides of the ship and scattered into spray as they broke on the steel bows. A breeze as heady as wine blew across the deck, arousing appetite in Della, so that directly she heard the breakfast gong she hurried to answer it and was soon entering the dining-room. She noticed at once that her table was empty and guessed that her companions of the night before would appear later or eat in their cabins. Joe Hartley had cracked a whole bottle of wine at dinner and probably had a 'head', and the honeymoon couple couldn't be expected to come down to earth, or the deck of a ship, just yet!

Music was coming from the tannoy, a catchy Italian song which seemed to match the sunlight, and Della was gaily ordering her breakfast when she caught the sound of a man whistling that lively tune as he strolled into the restaurant. He had such a melodic whistle that Della couldn't help but glance in his direction; a tall man in a dark silk shirt and impeccably cut off-white trousers, the strap of his gold watch glinting among the dark hairs of his brown arm.

'*Buon giorno, signorina.*' He paused beside her table

and looked all the way down at her with a quizzical air. 'Did you enjoy the film you saw last night?'

Della gazed all the way up at him with startled eyes. 'How do you know – I mean—'

'I know exactly what you mean.' He laid his hand over the back of the empty chair beside her. 'Do you think your companions of the table are likely to appear? If not, we could enjoy breakfast together.'

'Enjoy?' she murmured, and then as the music changed to a lively song from an operetta she knew well, she broke into an irrepressible smile which shaped her cheekbones and lips into a certain witchery and made the gem-like blue of her eyes more sunny and less icy. 'I notice your table companions have chosen to take breakfast in bed, and I do think it a pity to keep the waiter dashing from one half-empty table to another when we can share.'

'*Grazie.*' He sat down at the side of her and she noticed the lithe ease of his movements, and she caught a breath of his warm clean skin overlaid by a dash of tangy after-shave. She also realized that her pulses were beating at a far from normal rate, and that the atmosphere seemed to tingle with the undeniable magnetism of the man. As the waiter took his breakfast order, Della studied his profile. It had a strong Roman charm, with a thrusting authority to the clefted chin and the well-made nose. It was a face both subtle and primitive, combining the ancient lineage of him with the worldly instincts of a man who sought only pleasure from life and apologized to no one for his way of living.

Charm ... ruthlessness ... mockery. She saw them all in his face; she felt the danger that emanated from him, and she shivered a little as she let her eyes travel down his hard, brown arm overlaid by the dark hair of his maleness. If she now pushed back her chair and walked away from him she knew she would be safe ... but if she stayed . . .?

'Do you prefer the cinema to dancing?' he asked, and as he spoke his gaze was upon her fingers, which were tapping to the music being played. 'Or perhaps you are shy and feel the need to settle down before taking part in shipboard activities.'

'It was quite a good film,' she said. 'Anyway, how did you know I went to see a film last night? You were deep in conversation with a glamorous lady when I saw you last.'

'I have sharp eyes,' he drawled, sitting back in his chair and regarding her with those eyes, which also had the dark sensuous quality of the real Italian gaze, seeing women as women and not as opponents in a war of equal rights. 'I caught a glimpse of you on the lounge deck a moment before you concealed yourself in the shadows near the doors of the cinema. Lady of snow, from what are you running away?'

'Not a thing,' she denied swiftly, and was glad that in that moment the waiter brought her bacon and eggs to the table, and the Conte's grilled salmon roes on toast. 'Shall I pour your coffee, *signore*?'

'Grazie.' The sun flashed on his knife as he cut into his food.

'Cream and sugar?' She held the little jug poised above his cup.

'No cream, two lumps of sugar,' he said decisively.

'Of course.' She handed him his cup and there was no way of avoiding his eyes, until she swiftly dropped her gaze to that diamond scar on his cheekbone.

'All women wonder about it,' he said, a softly mocking note in his voice. 'It isn't a sign that I am one of nature's gamblers. It happened when I was a child; my nurse dropped me and I struck my face against the corner of a radiator, which was so hot that it acted like a branding iron. Do you find the mark ugly?'

'No – no, *signore*, of course not. It sets you apart – it's unusual, like the mark of a star.'

'Not the mark of a sinner?' he drawled. 'Italy has produced a fair proportion of sinners and saints, and I am sure you don't think of me as a saint.'

'You are Nicholas Franquila, one of the Casanovas of this world, are you not?' She smiled a little as she ate her bacon. 'I am sure that you chase Lady Fortune with all the enthusiasm with which certain English gentlemen chase the fox.'

'And which do you prefer, *signorina*, the fox-killer, or the lady-killer?' There was a smile quirking the edge of his mouth as he asked this question. 'Ah, I take one look into those wide eyes of yours – so exactly the colour of the sea – and I know the answer. You are a girl of ideals, and you have decided that I could never measure up to any of them. Well, I am not going to try, but I am going to ask you to give me some of your company while we are fellow travellers aboard the *Gothic Star*. Will you do that, Della Neve?'

'And why should you want me to, Count Nicholas?' With the artistry of her training Della imitated the seductive tones of the woman he had walked with last night, and probably kissed at the door of her stateroom. 'Do you find it necessary to make a willing victim of every woman on board?'

'Not every woman, *signorina*, only those who please my Italian eye.' And as he spoke in the deep, gravelly voice with the underplay of mockery, his eyes minutely examined her, taking in her thick fair hair at the nape of her neck, the pure line of jaw and throat, the silky skin over the fine collarbones revealed by the square neckline of her tunic. 'England is a land of roses, but you are one of the lilies, slim and cool and reserved.'

At his words, at his look, it took all of Della's coolness and acting ability to appear unimpressed. 'More coffee, *signore?*'

'If it has not become chilled,' he said dryly.

Their eyes met as she poured it, and they had to laugh. 'What are you afraid of?' he asked. 'That if you are seen with me your reputation will suffer?'

'It's possible, isn't it?' She thought fleetingly of Marsh, who would not regard this suave and slightly wicked *conte* as very good shipboard company for her. 'I expect there's a photographer aboard and you are fond of appearing in the papers with your conquests, are you not, *signore?*'

'Do you think you are about to become one of my conquests?' There was in the smile that flickered on his lips the audacity of a man who had never yet had any difficulty in getting his own way with a woman. 'Or do I glimpse a small shadow of fear in your eyes – fear of me, or of some other man who would not care to see your name linked with mine?'

He struck so uncannily close to the truth that Della almost cut her finger on the fruit knife she was using. Her nerves gave a jolt and the knife clattered on the plate and sent the rosy apple skittering in the Count's direction. He caught it adroitly, and Della looked at him with the wide and accusing eyes of a girl who felt herself at the mercy of a temperament never met with before, which drew her despite herself and scattered her composure and made her behave like a schoolgirl again.

'Why, *signorina*, do you plan to tempt me?' he drawled, with a significant look at the apple.

'No, *signore.*' She stood up with sudden decision and dropped her napkin to the table. 'I'm going off to the deck to sit with a book and I don't plan to tempt anything but some relaxation. I came on this cruise for the sake of my nerves, and you – you have a way of setting them all on edge. Good morning!'

'*Arrivederci, signorina.*'

Not if I can help it, she thought, and she marched out

of the restaurant in such a fury of determination that she almost collided with a lean figure in uniform. 'Sorry!' 'Oh, sorry!' they said in unison, and then he gave a slight laugh. 'You are brisk this morning, Miss Neve. Are you dashing off to join one of the deck games?'

'No, I'm off to get some sunshine.' She smiled back at him and recognized him as the young officer who had welcomed her aboard. 'It's such a gorgeous morning and I don't want to miss a breath of that sea air if I can help it. Can we expect this sort of weather to continue?'

'All the way to Zattere, according to the forecast.' His blue eyes regarded her with admiration from under the peak of his officer's cap. 'Will you be going to the dance tomorrow night, Miss Neve? The Captain always gives a landfall dance the night before we arrive in port and it's always a lively turnout. I thought – well, if you are planning to go, you might save me a few dances? As a fan of yours I'd be awfully honoured.'

'You're on, Lieutenant. I like to dance.'

'I'm sure you dance almost as well as you sing, Miss Neve. I only wish—'

Anticipating his wish Della lightly touched his sleeve. 'I didn't mean to be rude yesterday, but I'm under doctor's orders to rest my voice for a while. I'm very flattered that you enjoy my singing.'

'Along with lots of other people,' he said warmly. 'Well, I won't keep you from your deck-chair – my name, by the way, is Steve Ringdale, and it really is a great pleasure to meet you. If it doesn't sound too fulsome, I think you're the nicest person we have on the *Gothic* this trip.'

'How kind of you to say so – Steve.' Della was not confused by this young man as she had been by the man she had just left in the dining-room. He was so English and sincere that she couldn't help but like him. 'I'd like it if you would call me Della. On this trip I want to be just a holidaymaker and not a singer.'

'I understand – Della. Then I'll see you at the dance?'

'I shall look forward to it.' They smiled and parted, and before going to the upper deck Della went to her stateroom to collect a book and her writing-case. She would write to Marsh while she enjoyed the sun and let him know how good the weather was. In her absence everything had been made tidy and the water had been changed in the vase which held the white roses. As she lingered to admire them she thought of what the Conte had said about her, that she was more like a lily than the usual English rose. She was in no doubt that he had a store of phrases with which to flatter women, and with a touch of defiance she cut off a rosebud with her nail-scissors and pinned it to the collar of her tunic. It was as pretty as wax against the blue material, with that suggestion of innocence which Marsh had so carefully guarded in Della herself. It was the kind of innocence which she knew would act like a magnet to a woman-chaser, and so she wore Marsh's rose as a talisman against the pagan Nick and his dark attraction.

Up on the sun deck she found a secluded corner, where she proceeded to laze away the morning, with the sun warm on her legs and arms as she wrote her letter and read her book. Just around the corner from where she sat she could hear the children laughing and playing and splashing about in their very own pool. It was a carefree background to her thoughts, and there was the added assurance that sophisticated adults weren't likely to come up here.

Suddenly a child ran round the corner of the deck and then came to a halt as she caught sight of Della. A red ball rolled to Della's feet and she leaned over to pick it up and held it out to the child with a smile. The little girl hesitated and then came forward. 'I didn't know anyone was here,' she said. 'You did make me jump.'

'I am sorry about that, but I thought if I kept awfully quiet you children wouldn't mind me being here. I do hope you don't?'

'I don't mind.' The child approached a little nearer. 'Usually the grown-ups like to have fun with us out of their way. Are you a mother?'

Della shook her head and her smile deepened. 'No, I'm travelling all alone. This is a very nice ball, and you must make sure it doesn't roll into the sea.'

'Oh, my mother would buy me another,' the child said airily. 'She has lots of money, I think, for everyone says I never lack for anything because my father gave her lots of alley money when he went to live with Aunt Luella.'

'Alimony,' Della murmured, and she found herself wondering which woman on board was the divorced mother of this pretty child with the slightly sulky mouth.

'Can you swim?' the child asked. 'If this ship went down I wouldn't be able to swim and I would drown. I don't like the water. It frightens me and Momma gets mad with me. She says if I grow up to be a wilting Winnie she'll disown me.'

'I'm sure you'll grow up to be very pretty and lively,' said Della, and she wondered how a woman could treat a child's fears in such a flippantly cruel way. 'What makes you afraid of the water? It can be great fun when you learn to make a friend of it instead of an enemy.'

'It's all wet and clutchy and it tastes horrid.' The child gave a shudder and sat herself down on the foot of Della's deck-chair. 'Momma is never alone and likes lots of company, but she isn't all that fond of children. I'm going to stay with my grandpa and my aunt, who make wine and live among lots of grapevines. I shan't mind. It'll be better than being away at school all the time.'

Childish words which yet painted a very clear image of

a selfish woman who wished to enjoy life without having the bother of her small daughter.

'Look,' Della spoke impulsively, 'how about you and me going down to the café to have ice-cream and cake? I'm feeling peckish and would enjoy your company.'

'Pistachio with nuts?' The child leaned eagerly forward and the sun showed a dusting of freckles across her small nose. 'Do you mean it? I wouldn't be a bother?'

'Sweetheart, you'd be doing me a favour. I'm all on my lonesome, as you can see, and I don't care to go and eat ice-cream without someone to keep me company.'

'Why are you all alone?' The small fingers touched the rose on Della's tunic. 'Haven't you any boy-friends? Momma has lots, and she's older than you and she covers her face with a sort of pink cream out of a pot with a bee on the lid. She looks nice when she does that, but you look nice without anything on your face . . . all sort of smooth like rose petals. Are you divorced?'

'Heavens, no!' Della rose to her feet and gathered her belongings together. 'I'm not even married, and I do assure you that not all wives and husbands are unhappy together. It just means that a man and a woman must be right for each other and then nothing can go wrong and because they make each other happy, they make their children happy as well. Now how about telling me your name so we can be real friends?'

'I'm called Honey.' The child bit her lip. 'It's a silly name and the girls at school joke about it. They say I ought to be in a pot.'

'Well, I think it's rather pretty. It matches the colour of your hair, Honey. My name is Della, so now we've introduced ourselves we can go and have our ice-cream elevenses.'

Honey giggled and fell into step beside Della, but when they reached the brightly painted café they found it noisy and gay with lots of teenaged members of the cruise enjoying Cokes and ices at the cane-plaited tables. Della glanced round for a vacant table, but they were all occupied, so she bought big ice-cream cones for Honey and herself and they strolled along the promenade deck eating them. The child chatted about her grandfather and her widowed aunt, and Della gathered that their vineyard home was in Italy, and she couldn't help but think it a good idea that Honey be brought up there instead of being a boarding-school appendage of a mother who wished to renew her youth in a variety of flirtations with men.

Della and the child paused beside the rails to watch the sun making silver patterns on the water, while at the stern there streamed a multi-mile tail of foam, looking, Della remarked, like a great feather boa dropped overboard by a duchess.

Honey burst into young laughter, a trill of happy sound that pleased Della immensely. She was fond of young people, but her life with Marsh had rather excluded their companionship, and as she gazed at the eternally moving water she realized how much of her life had been spent with music masters, singing teachers, and all sorts of rather serious people involved in the world of classical music. She had not, after the age of ten, gone to school like other children but had learned her lessons with a tutor. Later on it had been Marsh himself who had taught her to be a composed and gracious young woman. A taste in good clothes had gradually been instilled into her. She had learned to appreciate all the arts, and to play a good hand at bridge. Her entire personality had been moulded by Marsh to suit his demanding and rather fastidious tastes, and Della felt again that spiral of rebellion making its way through her body as she stood at the rails of the *Gothic Star* and found how easy and enjoyable it was to amuse a child.

'Honey,' a voice suddenly carolled, 'what are you doing

down here? I told you to stay up on the sundeck until I came for you.'

Della and Honey turned from the rails at the same time, and Della immediately realized that the woman who companioned Nicholas Franquila was the mother of her new young friend, and here in daylight she looked as glamorous as she looked last night by starlight. She wore a pale orange denim blouse with full tucked sleeves held at the wrist by small buttoned cuffs. This was teamed with a suede skirt, and her dark hair was held in place by a filmy orange scarf. Her lips matched the scarf, and her almond-shaped eyes stared at Della with a disturbing animosity at their depths.

'Really, you've been feeding the child with ice-cream and now she'll eat no lunch! I do wish you well-meaning single women would leave the welfare of a child to its mother. Honey, you've that messy stuff all round your mouth and you look a perfect little sweep!'

'Oh, I don't know,' drawled the tall man at her side, and he was looking down at Honey with a pair of darkly smiling eyes,' your daughter is at the age, *signora*, when she can wear goo all over her mouth and still look fetching. I see, little one, that you have been enjoying the green pistachio ice-cream which I very much loved myself when I was your age.'

'Did they sell it all those years ago?' Honey asked him, her eyes huge and serious as they took in his lean, towering darkness.

'Oh yes,' he said, with equal seriousness. 'The pistachio ice-cream has been made in Italy since the days of Michelangelo, and there they sell it in the streets from coloured carts with parasols shading them.'

'That's all very well, Nick,' Honey's mother bent to wipe the remains of the ice-cream from the child's mouth, 'but if you had as much trouble as I have getting her to eat her meals you wouldn't talk that way. She has the appetite of a bird.'

'Well, you will both be lunching with me today, so I must try and coax Honey to eat like a young bear.' His gaze moved abruptly to Della, who found herself gripping the rail and steeling herself against the charm that was so lethal when he chose to destroy a woman's defences. 'It was kind of you to take Honey under your wing, Miss Neve. I expect Camilla is like most mothers and worries unduly when it comes to her offspring.'

'I'll take your word for it, *signore*.' Della couldn't keep a dry note out of her voice, and as his black eyebrows began to arch, she turned to Honey and bade her good-bye. 'It was kind of you, Honey, to keep me company. I hope we shall see each other again, and do be a good girl and eat your lunch.'

'Della—' Honey reached out for her, but Della walked on and couldn't look back at that expressive young face. She felt in her body the tension, the held-in anger against Camilla, who feigned such mother love and concern in front of 'one of her boy-friends', as Honey called them.

Della knew that it made her extra angry that the present boy-friend should be Nick Franquila. Despite the rumours that he was almost engaged to Sorine Hunter, he quite obviously couldn't stay away from other attractive women. Fury stabbed as Della thought of his conversation with her at the breakfast table ... if he imagined he was going to add her scalp to his belt, then he was in for a surprise. The ice-cold shoulder was due to the Conte, and Della appointed herself the person to do it. From now on Nicholas di Fioro Franquila was going to have some of his ego cooled down by the contempt of one woman at least!

It was at this point in her reflections that Della heard the patter of small feet running after her. 'Della ... Della ... I want to come with you!' a young voice cried out.

Della swung round and there was Honey running in

her wake, and striding behind Honey was the tall figure of the Conte. He swooped and caught hold of the little girl and swung her to his shoulder. He held her firmly there, while very deliberately he said to Della:

'You seem to have a way with you, *signorina.* A way of stealing the affections.'

'I don't mean to steal the affections of another woman's child.' Della gave him a cold look, and Honey a warm smile. 'I'll see you again, Honey, up on the sun-deck. But right now you must go and eat lunch with your mother and the *signore.*'

'I want to eat my lunch with you.' Honey struggled on the shoulder of her captor, but his lean hands were too strong for her and she could not escape . . . and there was Camilla hurrying to join the trio in her white cork-soled clogs. When she reached them her eyes blazed annoyance at Della.

'It's easy enough to seduce children by giving in to their every whim,' she said sharply. 'In future, Miss Neve, do you mind leaving my child alone?'

'Why, are you afraid that she might learn how to like a little kind understanding?' Della could not hold back the words. 'If Honey wishes to be friends with me, then I have no intention of ignoring her. I should like to add that she is less likely to learn selfish habits from me than from certain friends of yours.'

And with this parting barb, aimed at Nick Franquila, Della ran down the stairs to the main-deck and the colour was high on her cheekbones and her blue-green eyes sparkled with temper.

As she entered her stateroom and breathed the aroma of the white roses, she realized how alive she felt, and how involved in the emotional traumas of life.

The protective wall which Marsh had built around her was no longer there to keep her her from being hurt, and from fighting back when she was hurt. Now she was very much on her own, and she felt exhilarated by the way she had dealt with Camilla, and with Nick . . . the devil! He had stood there enjoying the encounter, the fair child high on his shoulder, and the demons of his amusement dancing behind the thick dark lashes of his Italian eyes.

Della's delicate brows gathered into a slight frown as she dropped her book and writing-case to the daybed. There was something about Nick Franquila from which she shrank, a ruthlessness, a strange awareness of something that made him hard and cruel . . . towards women. Yet she had to admit to herself that he had spoken to Honey as if he cared for children, and knew how to handle them.

The man was an enigma, she decided. He most definitely had a past, but she was one female on board this ship who didn't plan to delve into it.

Such delving struck her as foolhardy as diving over the side of the *Gothic Star* into the bottomless ocean . . . he was as deep as that . . . as dangerously enticing and destructive.

She read again the letter she had written to Marsh and added as a postscript that she was missing him very much. She added a kiss and knew he would smile his firm-lipped, rather serious smile and that look of indulgence would creep into his grey eyes. How very nice Marsh seemed in comparison to that dark Italian with secrets buried deep in his eyes. How safe, and how reliable, with all the future firmly arranged for her, with no pitfalls for her to stumble into.

She changed into a white piqué dress for luncheon, and walked to her table looking cool and composed. Joe Hartley rose at once to greet her. 'How nice you look, Miss Neve! You've put an edge on my appetite, just to look at you. Had no breakfast, y'see. Had a bit of a thick head.'

'Really, Mr. Hartley?' She smiled as she sat down. 'I

wonder what could have caused that? The sea air usually blows away all our cobwebs.'

He gave a hearty laugh and looked at her with shrewdly amused eyes as he sat down in the chair which had been occupied earlier by a much leaner and more sardonic man. 'Giving me a bit of charming chastisement, eh? I'll admit it, I do hit the bottle a trifle hard these days, but it's out of loneliness, my lass. There's nought harder than being lonely, and you're lonely in a crowd when you lose what's closest to you. Can't make out why a good-looking gal like yourself is taking a sea trip on your lonesome. Care to tell a man who's old enough to be your father?'

And so all through the meal Della talked to Joe about the present loss of her singing voice, while he talked about the loss of his much loved wife, and so absorbed were they in their conversation that to an observer it looked as if the willowy girl in white was fascinated by the middle-aged man with the rather worn face lit by a pair of sea-blue eyes.

At the end of lunch they left the dining-room together and went to the lounge-deck to drink their coffee.

Suddenly, as Joe clipped and set a flame to his cigar, he said something which shook Della more than she cared to show. 'Life's a long, bumpy road, my lass, and some of those bumps can shake us pretty hard. But a mighty big compensation along that road of life is the finding and the getting of the prize of real love from the right person. And it's a funny thing, lass, because that perfect partner is not always the way we imagine he, or she, ought to be. I make no pretence to good looks, not with my bulk and my balding pate, but my Maggie loved me, and she was pretty all her days. Could have had any man she looked at, but she took a shine to me and the gloss never wore off that shine, thank heaven. Well, what I'm saying to you, lass, is this. You'll never be truly happy with just a career, and I don't reckon for a moment that you've really lost your voice. What's going on inside you is a sort of rebellion against that career. I bet it's been your whole life up till now, making so many demands that you've never found time to have a real romance with someone.'

Joe leaned back in his cane chair and took a long pull at his cigar. 'If you were my daughter, and as I said before you're young enough and I'm old enough for such a relationship, I'd give you this advice. You have a bit of fun on this trip . . . there's no place like a ship for inducing feelings of romance, especially when the stars are shining, and you can take it from me that no man or woman really lived until the heart inside them turned over at a certain touch, or the sound of a certain voice. We just go through the motions of living, but it's love that brings us truly alive. You take my word for it. I had twenty-two years of true love, and I bet you're about that age but haven't yet felt that young heart of yours turn over, eh?'

Joe studied her face through the smoke he was making, then he said gruffly: 'It's been all music but no song in the heart, eh? Not yet, but it will happen, you mark my words.'

'But—' Della half-opened her lips to tell him that in six weeks she was to be married to a fine man, and then she swallowed the words, and they watched together through the curving lounge windows as a seabird came to the rail of the ship and hovered there like a white and black sculpture.

'Beautiful,' Joe murmured. 'Makes me wish I could paint.'

Della smiled, and thought that in his bluff way he wasn't bad at painting with words an epigram that lingered. 'It's been all music but no song in the heart, eh?'

She caught back a sigh as the graceful bird flew away

over the bright, silky water, for she knew what Joe meant . . . the silent, lovely, exciting song of the heart's rapture, heard and felt only by those who fell headlong in love . . . a devastating, emotional jolt to the senses which she had never felt . . . and might never be destined to feel, for her destiny lay with Marsh Graham.

'My Maggie never liked the water and that's why we never took a sea trip together.' Joe spoke with a gruff note of sadness in his voice. 'Then in the strangest way it was getting soaked to the skin that led to her death. She ran out in the pelting rain to fetch in a hurt bird from our garden and she didn't stop to put on a coat or a pair of overshoes. She took a chill and within twenty-four hours pneumonia set in, and she proved allergic to the drugs they used and she died. I ask why a good deed should be repaid in that way; why a kind and unselfish soul like Maggie should just close her eyes and be gone, lost to a man in that marble sleep. Surely it's here on earth where we need the angels; heaven by now must have its share of those after two world wars and a dozen minor ones. There's no doubt about it, lass. Life is a hard and bumpy road to travel.'

'But let's hope,' she leaned forward and pressed his hand, 'that for the next few weeks the sea runs smooth for us.'

Joe smiled at her words and his fingers reversed and had hold of hers, and they were sitting thus, in a friendly silence, when a man strolled past the windows of the lounge and happened to glance in at the couple in the window seat. His dark eyes narrowed and stared, and in that moment Della glanced up and met the gaze that seemed to penetrate the glass, burning through it to bring a sudden heat to her cheeks. Then he quirked an eyebrow in that inimitably mocking way of his and walked on along the deck, leaving in his wake the smoke of his cheroot, a small cloud in the sunlight.

CHAPTER THREE

DELLA dressed for the dance that took place the night before landfall, applying her favourite perfume before slipping into a champagne-coloured gown with full romantic sleeves and a soft neckline. She had been to the Purser to collect her jade necklace and matching bracelet, but once again she had left the ring to be locked away. She turned from the mirror to avoid her own eyes, and slipped her feet into her gold-coloured dancing shoes.

Joe Hartley had asked to escort her to the ballroom, where a buffet was to be laid on for those who didn't wish to sit down to dinner, but when the little chime on her clock struck nine, Della decided that he had forgotten all about her and was probably enjoying the company of a bottle of wine. She took up her silk cloak and swung it about her shoulders and decided to go to the ball on her own. The young officer Steve Ringdale would be there, and tonight she felt like dancing and losing her cares in the music and the laughter.

As she made her way along the carpeted corridor to the stairs, she was unaware that she had the look of a lovely ghost. Her golden shoes made no sound on the blue carpet, and her cloak shimmered softly about her slim figure. Her aspen-gold hair was drawn back softly from her brow, the wide sweep of her fine dark eyebrows, and jewel-bright eyes. Her mouth was softly painted, and facial make-up intensified the clear beauty of her features.

She smiled a little to herself as she mounted the stairs, for this part of the ship seemed deserted and she might have been the only passenger on board ... an illusion abruptly dispelled as she rounded a bend and saw the silhouette of a man against the ship rails, outlined by the stars that were let loose in the sky in great silver clusters, reflecting in the sea so that it glittered like frosted glass.

The sudden sight of another human being startled Della and she gave a little gasp . . . at once he swung to face her, clad in a white tuxedo, black narrow trousers, and a wine-red tie above the starched ruffles of a white dress shirt. His lean face had the distinction of a fine sculpture, and his black hair was as well groomed as his graceful body. And he stood there in his raking darkness like a sort of inevitable threat to Della as she crossed his path.

A little wind blew off the sea and brushed her throat, and she told herself that was why she shivered.

'So it is you, *signorina.*' His words broke the silence, spoken in that faintly accented voice like dark honey strewn with gravel. 'For a few seconds you looked almost unearthly and I thought I was being haunted by a ghost.'

'Why should you be afraid of ghosts, *signore*?' Della just managed to keep her voice steady. 'Surely only sinners carry that fear about with them.'

'What makes you so sure that I am a sinner?' He began to approach her, treading as silently as if he walked on velvet paws. 'Are you one of those so far sheltered English girls who believe that a man of foreign appearance is automatically a rake? I could be less so than the fatherly type who lulls you into a false sense of security, patting your hand and smiling with a tired charm, as if all desire is spent and he needs only a daughter.'

'You have a cruel tongue!' she exclaimed. 'If you're referring to my friendship with Mr. Hartley, then it might interest you to know that he recently lost his wife, whom he loved very much, and he is sincerely in need of sympathy. You wouldn't understand what it feels like to love someone, or to miss them so much that it hurts.

You're too wrapped up in yourself and your own pleasures—'

'*Mia*, you are getting so het up that some of your English ice might melt at any moment.' Swiftly he reached for her and took her by the shoulders and she found herself as helpless in his grip as Honey had been the other day. It would be an indignity to struggle with him, for not only would she be the loser, but her dress and her hair would be disarranged and she had taken such pains with her appearance. Temper flared in her eyes as she flung back her head and looked at him. With her every fibre she wanted to hate him, but the vibrations from his touch and his closeness were not those of repugnance. They were electrifying, as if all at once her body had come into contact with a vital force beyond the control of her mind. A force of strength and personality that made her knees go weak, a most alarming sensation which filled her eyes with a look of shock as they fixed themselves upon his dark, distinctive, and threatening face.

As he read her eyes a little flame of satanic amusement kindled in his eyes. 'You must be a little innocent if you judge people by what is written about them by malicious gossips in the tabloids,' he said. 'Would it not be kinder of you – and I feel sure you are a kind girl at heart – to get to know me before you presume to judge me? There is every chance that I might strip your soul to its long white gloves, but there is also the chance that we might become – friends. Won't you take a chance and see what develops, Lady of Snow?'

'What do you mean – take a chance?' She stood between his hands with all the dignity she could muster, in view of the crazy trembling of her knees. What the devil was the matter with her? She had not reacted like this when she had sung for her first opera producer; she had been cool and in complete control of her limbs and there had not been a quaver in her voice.

'Let down your guard, *signorina*. Let yourself enjoy my company – if I am not totally obnoxious to you. Am I?'

As he asked this question Della felt his eyes upon her hair and her face. *Felt* them as opposed to merely being looked at by a man. It was her own disturbing reactions to his personality which shook her so much – after all, she had lived in close contact with a forceful man for a dozen years and should be as unshaken as the wall of China by this Latin playboy.

'I am sure you have had too many successes with women to care very much what I think of you,' said Della. 'I am also convinced that you know your own degree of attraction and wouldn't care very much if I found you unattractive. Personally speaking I prefer fair-haired men.'

'I am not asking you to fall in love with me,' he rejoined, an edge of mockery to his voice. 'I am merely asking you to come and dance with me – and later on, around midnight perhaps – I may ask you to spend tomorrow with me, when we go ashore to see one of the wonders of my country, Venice.'

'What about Camilla? Is she making up a third?' Della couldn't keep a tart note out of her voice, for he had spent a fair amount of cruising time in the company of the attractive divorcee and her young daughter. 'Or are you feeling in need of a change?'

At once his fingers dug into her shoulders and she flinched before she could stop herself.

'I have asked you to come and see Venice with me because I had the idea, perhaps a mistaken one, that you would be more receptive to its ancient beauties than Camilla, who is a thoroughly modern-minded woman. I believe this to be your first visit to Venice and I thought to act as your guide, unless you have already made arrangements to see the bride of the sea with your friend Mr. Hartley?'

In a flash Della was tempted to say that she was going to spend the forthcoming day with Joe, but even as the words came to her lips, a stronger compulsion took hold of her. A compulsion beyond her control and one she would surely regret later on.

'It's quite true, *signore*. I have never visited Venice before and it would be interesting to see the place with someone who knows it well. Guided tours are not quite my cup of tea.'

'I thought not, *signorina*.' His hands relaxed on her shoulders, but they didn't withdraw and Della tautened as she felt his fingers stroking the silk of her dress, which was of such a fineness that she felt as if he were stroking her skin itself. 'I can almost feel your bones, Miss Neve. Tomorrow we must dine on some of the local dishes and get a little flesh on your frame.'

'I do apologize, *signore*, for not being as plump as a Latin woman,' she retorted, and her voice was a little on edge after that startling touch of his fingers . . . more of a caress than an exploration of her fine-boned shoulders.

'No girl could be so different from an Italian woman,' he drawled, a sardonic amusement in the Latin eyes glinting down at her in the mingled starlight of sky and sea. 'It is like comparing the moon to the sun. The sun is warm and so it seems close to us, but the moon is silvery cool and often in hiding. Ah yes, you seem far more like Diana the moon goddess than you are like the golden sun. Far more difficult to reach; far less generous with your warmth. You are well named, Della Neve.'

'My real name is Dolly,' she said on impulse. 'It was changed to Della for professional reasons – and now shall we go to the ballroom, *signore*?'

'You are impatient for us to dance together?' he drawled.

'No! I happen to fancy a sandwich and a drink. I am not an airy-fairy creature who can dance on a lettuce leaf, for all that you think me skinny.' With a haughty flourish of her cloak Della made along the deck to where light was streaming out from the glass-panelled doors of the ballroom; music was playing and people were chattering, but there was a momentary silence as Della entered the room with Nicholas di Fioro Franquila, looking every inch the Latin aristocrat, and with a slight smile on his lips that indicated he was feeling pleased with life.

Greetings were called out to him, but he merely inclined his head and gave all his attention to Della by removing her cloak and revealing her in her pale-gold dress, by handing the cloak to an attendant and letting it be seen that he was her escort.

There was bound to be comment, and a few heads turned to catch the reaction of a certain brunette wearing a sleek and shimmering red dress with black velvet piping around the bodice and the medieval sleeves. Her painted eyes glittered like the jewels in her ears as she met the slightly malicious glances of those who had begun to think that she had captivated the Conte. But his sudden appearance at the side of the reserved English singer seemed to indicate that he had grown bored with the attractive divorcee and had switched his attention to the lovely, cool, fair creature who had so far spent her time in the company of the bluff Northern businessman who looked old enough to be her father.

On any cruising ship a certain amount of gossip and speculation goes on as to who will fall in love with whom during the course of the trip, and Della, as she accepted a glass of Romani Conti from Nick's hand, was well aware of the glances being shot at her and the man who stood selecting his own sandwich after serving her with turkey-breast on thin slices of rye bread.

Della tried to look unconcerned as she ate her sandwich and sipped her wine, but she was inwardly perturbed. There was every chance that someone on board knew of her association with Marsh Graham, and she hated the thought of gossip filtering back to him. After all, she had not done a thing to encourage Nick, and had been the reverse of the usual come-hither female of his acquaintance. Perhaps it was her reserve which had challenged him, but right now she could do nothing about shaking him off. Having entered the ballroom with him, she must now behave as casually as if he were Joe, or Steve Ringdale.

In that moment she caught sight of Steve among the dancers, and she gave him a quick smile. He held a young blonde in his arms and after returning Della's smile he shot a look at Nick's wide shoulders which spoke volumes. Even in dress uniform Steve indicated that he didn't feel up to competing with the Conte, and Della realized that this attitude would be general among the men at the dance, and tonight she would find herself the exclusive partner of Nick Franquila.

She met his eyes, and his eyebrow arched and his lip quirked.

'Camilla is looking gorgeous,' she said, deliberately. 'Aren't you being cruel to neglect her in front of all these people? They know you've been courting her.'

'I've spent a little time with her,' he contradicted Della, the quirk to his lip deepening. 'But when a woman begins to act as if she owns me, then I react like the hermit-crab and retreat to my shell. It is the Latin in me, *signorina.* Though I have lived in America for the past few years I remain Italian. You comprehend?'

'Indeed,' she said dryly. 'You like to do the chasing; you prefer to call the tune.'

'Yes, and I like very much the tune which the orchestra is now playing. You know it?'

Della glanced across the baroque ballroom to where the members of the orchestra had broken into a waltz, *Schöne Rose*, so lovely, so evocative of Vienna and the candlelit days when lovers had danced all through the night.

'Come, lovely Doll, dance with me.' Nick held open his arms and Della entered them in a sudden mood that desired movement, harmony, a few minutes of being wafted back to the days of romance. She felt Nick's arms tighten about her, holding her to his tall, lithe body as they danced. She had guessed that he would be a good dancer as he was a Latin, but what she had not foreseen was her own response to him as a partner. She loved to dance but had always found Marsh a rather stiff and formal partner whenever they had danced together at a supper club, or at the home of one of his business associates.

But Nick was neither stiff nor formal; he had grace, an instinctive response to the rhythm of the music, and he held Della as if she were part of him so their steps matched perfectly and each turn, each variation in the waltz was a delight she could not deny.

As the waltz neared its end, Della knew that Nick signalled to the orchestra leader, and instead of going into something modern the musicians kept on playing Strauss music and soon the dance floor was crowded with couples, young and old, drifting in from other parts of the ship, from the cinema and the smoke room and the tavern, where the teenagers usually flocked. It was as if a note of nostalgia had been struck into life, and soon the dancers had spilled out on to the deck and were performing the polkas, mazurkas and waltzes under the stars that swarmed in the sky.

'Nick.' Della spoke suddenly, a fine flush across her cheekbones and a sparkle in her eyes. 'You are possessed of a sort of wizardry, aren't you? You lift your finger and everyone falls under your spell.'

'Not mine, *nina*. These people are under the spell of the inimitable master of music, the great Strauss, Johann the son.'

'But you were the one who signalled the orchestra to go on playing his gorgeous music. What a surprise! I thought you the great sophisticate, Nick.'

'You think too much, Dolly,' he mocked, and with adroit ease he waltzed her out of the ballroom and along the deck until they came to a corner and he whirled her around it into the sudden hush and the play of the soft night breeze rising off the calm silver sea. They were now in semi-tropical waters and the stars seemed bigger, more like diamonds than the frost motes that glittered over northern waters.

Della stood speechless at the rails of the ship and felt her entire person humming with the loveliness of the night, and with the music of another time. She had never felt so alive, and yet so still, as if like a star she were suspended on that Milky Way to the palace of heaven. She felt ravished by the beauty of everything, aware of Nick beside her, and yet unaware of the shining elegance of her own person in the starlight.

Nick was as silent as she, gazing at the ocean as if seeing a memory there. They no longer touched and were held apart for the first time in hours by the enticement of the star-made shadows, silver and velvet. A remotenes had fallen upon him, which mystified and fascinated her. The pallor of his tuxedoed arm lay within reach of her hand, and yet he seemed a thousand miles away, lost in the depths of his thoughts as his eyes dwelt on the sea far below where they stood. The music drifted faintly to them, and Della slowly turned her head so she could see the starlight on his profile, not softening but defining something almost pagan in the shape of his bones, in the slant of his black eyebrow, in the clefting of his chin.

She had been determined to think of Nick as a cynical *roué*, seeking his worldly pleasure at the expense of other people, but tonight she had danced in his arms and felt him to be far more human than she had believed. He had sensed from *Schöne Rose* that the dance could be elevated from the ordinary to the highly enjoyable and he hadn't hesitated to use the influence attached to his title, not merely to amuse himself but to please a large number of people.

Suddenly he stirred and his eyes had captured Della's gaze before she could withdraw it. 'We both heard him, eh? The angel of silence.'

She nodded. 'Chekhov described it beautifully, that small silence that we somehow fear to break. Do you think an angel really does fly by?'

'How would a sinner know?' he murmured, a little wickedness creeping back into his eyes. 'Angels and devils don't keep company as a rule; it makes for an uneasy relationship when the angel is trying to pin wings on the devil, who is doing his best to strip the wings off the angel.'

'Like a naughty boy pulling the wings off a moth,' she murmured. 'What drives you to it, Nick? You can be – nice.'

'Nice?' He laughed with soft irony in the starlight. 'Yes, when it suits me, but not when it suits other people. That is the difference between a sinner and a saint.'

'But doesn't it feel *good*, Nick, to be good? Being bad can only sour the soul.'

'I am not interested in souls – least of all the soul of a lovely woman. I live for today, *nina*. For tonight – look how the stars over the sea create the illusion that the water is all limpid innocence. You and I are really aware that if this ship went down at this moment, all that heavenly loveliness would turn to hell.'

'Oh, how cynical you are!' Her hands gripped the rail, as if she felt the sway of the ship and the stab of fear that it was tipping over. 'Now you've spoiled all my pleasure in tonight!'

'The pleasure of the dancing is already a memory,' he

said, and there was a strange moody note in his voice. 'Yesterday is already a memory, for it is now midnight. Doll, will you spend tomorrow with me, if I promise to be as nice as I am capable of being?'

Della gazed at the sea and still felt shaken by the cruel way he had shattered her mood of delight in the dancing and the night. Instinct warned her to refuse him, to walk away now, and forget that for an instant she had caught a flare of pain in his eyes when he had talked of yesterday being but a memory. Was it possible that a sadness lay in Nick's past; a memory of which he never spoke but which haunted him on a night such as this, now the music was still and the stars hovered in silent, eternal witness to all sins and all sorrows?

Her heartbeats quickened, for the stars over the sea created a dangerous aura of romance, and she was such a novice when it came to dealing with a man such as Nick Franquila. 'I – I can't decide right now,' she said, backing away from his tall, dark figure. 'Let's wait until the morning, for you may be in a different mood by then and may wish to accompany someone else–'

'Be quiet!' His hand shot out and gripped her by the wrist, and the moody charm was banished from his eyes and replaced by a glittering anger. 'I want your answer right now, so is it yes or no, and I assure you it won't keep me awake if you say you can't keep me company when we go ashore tomorrow. I merely thought it might be enjoyable, but if you think otherwise then you are at liberty to say so. I shan't toss you over the side of the ship for having a will of your own.'

'My liberty feels threatened,' she said. 'Do you have to take hold of my wrist as if you'd like to break it?'

'You should beware of arousing temper in an Italian, *signorina*. He is not such a cool customer as your Englishman.'

'My Englishman?' Her pulses leapt and for a shocked

little moment she wondered if he knew about Marsh.

'Don't tell me, *signorina*, that you have been so sheltered that you have never had an English boy-friend.' His cynical eyes swept her from head to toe. 'You dance a little too well, and dress a lot too well, to be able to protest that you have never been courted. In my life I have sometimes met the career woman and she has a certain diamond hardness which you have not. You are much more the opal type, with a chameleon quality to you, a changing aspect from morning to night. The career woman has a way of keeping to the same trend of thought, the same hairstyle, the same style of costume. That is why the true career woman gets along so well in business, because the men with whom she deals can be certain that she will not suddenly change from a totally calm and collected person to a flushed, struggling pretty moth, more than a little afraid of life. When first I saw you, Dolly Neve, I thought you might well be one of these total ice maidens, but no icy careerist melts for a child, or gets furious with a mere man. She is above all that, with three-quarters of herself submerged like an iceberg. She doesn't feel as you do, *nina.* She is not emotional enough to care whether a man is nice or nasty. Whether he goes to the devil or the angels.'

'And you think I care where you are going?' Della stormed. 'And do stop calling me Dolly! My name has been changed and I prefer it that way!'

'I shan't ask who changed your name for you – in fact, I shall ask no questions except one.' He gazed down at her and she saw from his eyes that she intrigued him as much as he intrigued her. He was like no other man she had ever been allowed to meet, and she was probably a rare female in his view because she didn't throw herself into his arms. As she felt his fingers pressing into her wrist the jades which Marsh had given her, she wondered what he would say if she suddenly told him that she was engaged to one of the richest men in England; a man so kind, so protective, that in all but body she already belonged to him and could not allow the physical attraction of another man to blind her to Marsh's superior qualities of mind and character.

Marsh could give her protection and security all her life . . . a man like Nick could only fill her eyes with star-shine and break her heart as he had doubtless broken other hearts.

'What is in a name anyway?' Nick lifted her wrist and studied the gems encircling them. 'Woman is a mixture of Madonna and Melisande, and it is according to the man she is with, it is his effect upon her which will bring out the angelic or the daring. Nothing is more deceptive than the appearance of a person, and right now you remind me of a Florentine portrait in that charming gold dress, with your pale hair drawn away from your wide eyes and the definition of your cheekbones, softly shadowed to the soft fullness of your lips. A man of collective instincts would be unable to resist adding you to his gallery of valuable objects, no doubt as the lovely centre-piece.'

'I find your kind of flattery too sardonic to be sincere,' she said, and again a thread of shock ran through her body as his fingers seemed to press with secret meaning against the jade bracelet. 'In fact, I don't ask for flattery from any man.'

'All the same, it's nice to get it, eh?'

'If the compliment is meant kindly.'

'And you doubt my kindness? You think I have an ulterior motive in admiring your appearance? Come, do you think I plan to steal the Mona Lisa when I stand in front of it at the Louvre and feel a thrill of national pride that a countryman of mine painted the glorious thing? As a matter of fact I have not the collector's instinct. I like to look, to touch, and then I walk on to the next charming object. I prefer to travel lightly and my way of life can be enjoyable. I never ask a woman to share it, only to participate for an hour, or a day.'

'Does Sorine Hunter know that?' Della couldn't resist asking.

'Sorine is like her name,' he laughed softly. 'She also collects trophies, but my head belongs on my own shoulders, and I like my pelt just where it is, on my own back.'

'Is the rogue tiger running away from the huntress?' Della quipped.

'No,' he said, and the smile at the edge of his mouth was both mocking and a little cruel. 'I am bored with the new world and I am returning to the old one. I want to smell the cypress trees again, to which the nightingales come on a still night. I desire Italy more than I desire any woman.'

And strangely enough Della believed him and saw again in his eyes that flare of pain that drew him back to Italy as, perhaps, it had once sent him away.

'Are you wondering why I take the long route when I could have taken a jet?' he asked. 'The truth is that I was going to, and then while I was in England for a few days on business, a friend of mine who was taking this cruise fell ill and I took over his booking. The little things of fate, *signorina.* We should not have met but for my friend's attack of jaundice.'

'Jaundice?' she exclaimed, and thought of Julius Bolt, the conductor friend of Marsh's who was to have taken this cruise and would, as Marsh had said with his serious smile, have kept a friendly eye upon her. But no, it must be a coincidence. Marsh and Nick Franquila weren't likely to know the same kind of people, least of all people in the musical world. It was just an odd little stroke that jaundice should attack Julius.

'Your face has the pallor of night flowers,' Nick murmured. 'I think I must allow you to go to bed, but first I will have my answer with regard to seeing part of my homeland together. Do you wish for this or not?'

'Yes – why not?' Della spoke on impulse, and thrust the thought of Marsh to the back of her mind. After all, what harm could come of spending a day in Venice with a man who needed, though he didn't put it into words, a sensitive appreciation of the dying charms of the ocean's bride?

'What time would you like me to be ready in the morning?' she asked.

'The ship will arrive at Zattere about seven o'clock, so make it as early as possible. I shall come for you at the door of your stateroom and we can go ashore to eat breakfast at a café on the Piazzetta.'

'I shall enjoy that, *signore*. Until the morning then.'

'Allow me to escort you to your room—'

'I have to collect my cloak from the ballroom—'

'Please wait here and I will bring it to you.'

Della watched as he strode away and went out of sight around the corner of the deck, and now she was alone she felt a sudden coolness in the air, a sea breeze that touched her bare neck and stirred the silk of her dress. Several minutes passed and Della decided to follow Nick to the ballroom. She had half-turned the deck when she came to an abrupt halt and drew back swiftly into the shadows. Nick's height, and the shimmer of pale silk over his arm, made him unmistakable. The face of the woman who stood so close to him could not be seen, but Della felt certain it was Camilla who detained him and held him in low-voiced conversation. Della gave a shiver, half of cold and half of annoyance. Well, she wasn't going to stand around here developing a chill while he resumed his flirtation with Camilla, and turning on her heel Della fled away in the direction of the stairs, her sleeves of transparent silk billowing like wings that seemed to carry her swiftly to her stateroom. She closed the door with a curt finality behind her, and she refused to open it when he finally came and drummed his knuckles against the panels.

'Go away!' she muttered, as she kicked off her dancing shoes. And as if he heard her words he went, and when she dared to open the door she found her cloak carefully folded on the blue carpet. As she picked it up a slip of paper fell from the silky folds. She was half inclined to rip the note into pieces, but curiosity overcame her flash of temper and she read the words he had written on a small page torn from a pocketbook – his book of telephone numbers, no doubt!

'Buon riposa,' she read. 'Until *domani.* Nick.'

The nerve of the man! Did he really imagine – and then Della bit her lip and realized that he would keep her to the promise she had made with regard to their day together. Camilla, he had said, was thoroughly modern-minded, which meant that old buildings lichened from centuries of lapping water were not *her* glass of wine! Della on the other hand, being slightly old-fashioned, would be bound to enjoy the waterworn *palazzos,* the marble statues and the many bridges, under which the black and creaking gondola would glide, manned by a Venetian in a striped jersey.

The trouble was her own certainty that she would enjoy all these things, and she didn't much like the idea of being one of a group, hustled from one place to another before she had time to absorb the beauty and history of one of the world's most legendary cities.

Della felt a sense of dilemma as she prepared for bed, but it wasn't until she was turning off the lamp that she was struck by a disturbing thought . . . was it jealousy she had felt up there on the deck, seeing Nick with another woman just after he had spent the best part of the evening dancing with her?

Was that why she had flounced off to her stateroom

and refused to open the door to his knock?

Her cheeks suddenly burned and she buried her face in her pillows. Dash the man! He had come like a catalyst into her carefully planned life, and she felt certain his vast amount of experience would have told him why she had flounced off without saying good night to him. She tightly closed her eyes and willed herself to forget about him, but such was the charisma of the man that still she heard his voice, still she saw his face, and only by falling asleep was she able to escape from him.

When Della awoke in the morning she felt at once the stillness of the ship and guessed at once that they were at rest in the harbour of Zattere. She tossed aside the bed-covers and ran to the nearest porthole, which framed a scene that made her catch her breath. There on the blue water bobbed the painted boats and the black, high-prowed gondolas, and it was like looking at an animated photograph.

They were now in Italy and Della told herself that from now on she must adopt a *dolce far niente* attitude of mind and not worry if she could help it. Did they not call Venice the city of consolations, where one's troubles could be drowned for a while?

In that instant there came a tap at the door and she froze for a second or two, until a key-ring rattled and Larkin cheerfully entered carrying a tray on which stood coffee and biscuits. He took the liberty of winking as he set the tray down on the table. 'The Count said you'd be needing these, miss, as you'd be going ashore early. You have a nice day for sightseeing, for sometimes when we've put into port here there's been a mist hanging over the lagoon. Special sort of place is Venice, not like any other city, with something a bit sad and nostalgic about it. You know, like an actress who's been terrific in her day but is now falling apart. You'll like Venice, Miss Neve. Especially them dashing gondoliers with their tenor voices!'

Della smiled and tied the sash of her robe. She tried to appear quite cool about the Conte, and even said casually: 'It will be very interesting to see the city in the company of an Italian, and I must admit that I'm looking forward to going ashore – or rather afloat.'

'Funny way of living, isn't it, miss?' Larkin grinned. 'Doing your shopping by boat, and having your bread delivered in a basket. I don't know what my missus would say to such an arrangement. Well, I wish you a happy day, Miss Neve.'

'Thank you, Larkin.'

After the steward had gone Della drank her coffee and ate a couple of biscuits, still standing there by the porthole which framed the sea-green ocean and the blue sky. It was kind of magical, she thought, the way the sea had taken on that green tinge so that the water seemed to mirror with greater clarity the coloured sails of the fishing boats, and the gilded prows of the gondolas that stood in a line along the shore, many of them with strange emblems painted on the 'neck' of the boat, either as decoration or as some sort of charm against storms.

Then as her little clock chimed Della realized that she had better bathe and dress for her sightseeing tour with the Conte. She hurried into the bathroom and took a shower, after which came the problem of what to wear for the day. Later on the sun would be really warm, so after inspecting her wardrobe Della selected a dress of white eyelet embroidery, so simple to look at until she put it on, when against her lightly sea-tanned skin the dress became rather stunning. Pleased with her fresh, crisp look, Della arranged her hair into a chignon and stabled the glossy gold bun with a jade pin. She then applied a light make-up, slipped her feet into piqué court shoes, tipped the contents of yesterday's handbag into a piqué purse, sprayed on a lily-of-the-valley perfume and felt ready for any encounter.

It was as she was pulling on the dusty-pink gloves which matched her shoes and bag that Della took a long, reflective look at her bare left hand.

In the beginning she had left off her ring in a mood of slight rebellion against the sternly tender restraints which Marsh had imposed upon her. But right now instinct was warning her that it was becoming rather dangerous not to wear her engagement ring, and she had almost decided to go and collect it from the Purser when there came a tap upon her door and she knew from the leaping of her nerves who had come to call for her.

Masking her nervous tension with an air of composure Della walked to the door and opened it. '*Buon giorno,*' he said, and he took in her appearance in one dark sweep of his eyes. '*Bene,* I see you are all ready and waiting!'

'Good morning, *signore.*' She restrained herself from looking him over and kept her eyes upon his face. 'I didn't wish to keep you waiting, for I know how impatient men become with women who dilly-dally over their *toilette.* I imagine it will be quite warm later on, so I hope I have dressed sensibly?'

Again his dark eyes flicked her slender figure in the crisp white dress complemented by her dusty-pink accessories, running down the slim length of her legs and up again to her pale hair, her blue-green eyes, and her softly painted lips.

'The word sensible does not apply,' he said, with a slight smile.

'Oh – do you think I'm all wrong for a day out in Venice?' As always she couldn't quite fathom his smile and what lay behind it. 'It wouldn't take me long to change, if you care to wait—'

'I would not have changed a hair on your head, *signorina,* nor a single item of what you are wearing. You look *bellissima,* and I shall have to guard you well from the roving eye and hand of my fellow Italians. I would suggest, however, that if you have a sunhat it will save you from the hot rays of the sun when it burns down on the water. I have already secured for us a gondola and we shall do a tour of the Grand Canal after we have had breakfast.'

She turned quickly away from him so he wouldn't see how the colour rose to her cheeks at his compliment. How much more meaningful it sounded to be called beautiful in Italian! Marsh had often admired her appearance, but in a way which had pleased her without making her feel shy and confused. She knew herself attractive without being vain about it, but Nick made her feel as if never before had a man really looked at her, seeing not only a pleasing image but the shape of her bones, the arrangement of her features, the colour and texture of her hair and her skin.

Her hand shook slightly as she opened the built-in wardrobe and took from the hat shelf a brimmed straw with a high crown decorated by a bunch of artificial cherries.

'Will this do?' She braced herself to face Nick and showed him the hat, which she had bought the other day in one of the ship's boutiques for wearing on deck when she sunbathed. Having such a fair skin she had to be careful not to burn, and the ridiculous hat had taken her fancy because it was so far removed from the chic type of hats which she normally wore.

She half expected Nick to burst out laughing, but instead he said the hat was charming and exactly right for Venice. 'There is nothing solemn about the bride of the sea. She is gay and a little amoral and does not approve of those who are too formal. Her motto might well be *cercàre la vita*. Seek life, don't run away from it.'

'I am sure, *signore*, that you have taken it for your own motto,' she said, and as she preceded him from her stateroom and turned to lock the door after them, she felt the look he was giving her, slightly mocking and sardonic and at the same time admiring. She warned herself that he knew all the tricks of getting under the skin of even the most worldly woman, and she, despite her career as a singer, was not a woman who knew much of men. The motto of Marsh was that work came before pleasure.

But Della couldn't suppress her own sense of pleasure when the firm hand of Nick assisted her into the gondola which was to take them across the *laguna*. A water-worn but lovely old craft, decorated with gilded sea-horses at either side of the seats. These seats each had a single arm and were made comfortable with fringed cushions of red silk. The gondolier as he took up his stance and lifted the great oar from its carved rest had a look of sun-darkened grace in a loose white shirt, dark trousers and a red-striped bandana about his head.

As the oar struck the water and they moved away gracefully from the jetty where the *Gothic Star* was moored, Della relaxed in her seat and let the *dolce far niente* feeling sweep over her. 'You think too much,' Nick had said, and it was true. The time had come for feeling, and she smiled and thanked Nick for this her first trip in a gondola.

'One should always see Venice for the first time in a gondola,' he said, very much at his ease in his seat, the light grey of his suit making even more emphatic the dark distinction of his looks. 'It would be unromantic for you, Della Neve, to arrive in a water bus like any ordinary visitor to Venice.'

'But I am only an ordinary visitor,' she said lightly. 'You don't have to pay me the usual charming compliments, *signore*. I shall be quite happy to be treated as a tourist lucky enough to have a knowledgeable guide. You don't have to – romance me just because Venice is one of the most romantic cities in the world.'

'Would it not make a happy change for you to be – romanced?' he drawled. 'Always there is something a little serious about you, as if you are afraid to let yourself be young. I am going to guess that you have had imposed upon you this serious air and that beneath it there lurks a hidden gaiety. I warn you that the insidious magic of Venice will search it out and bring it to the surface and after today. Lady of Snow, you may never be the same again.'

CHAPTER FOUR

'You—' Della took a deep breath of recovery, 'you make that prediction sound more like a threat.'

'Do I?' He gave her a suave smile. 'That is because I know the witchery of Venice, and I know the vulnerability of a woman.'

'You will not find me vulnerable,' Della rejoined, and as she looked away from his worldly, knowing eyes, she caught her first glimpse of San Marco, the sun on the marble columns of the *campanile*, with hundreds of birds flying around the wondrous cluster of domes and towers. And she heard the bells ringing across the blue-green water, as if every day in Venice were the blessed day of Sunday.

'How very lovely!' The words came softly from her lips, like a prayer, and she knew the wand of entrancement touched her as they glided nearer all the time to the great stone mansions and the strange narrow houses that grew out of the sea itself, as if by magic, and her heart whispered that this was a city to which the lonely came, and the lovers. It cast an undeniable spell, for the beauty of it all was trapped in the water, softened by the ever-moving mirror of the sea, the scars of time made less harsh in the warmth of the Italian sun.

The sun flashed on the mosaic cupolas of San Marco, the great cathedral of Venice, and Della caught her breath in wonder. 'So very beautiful, so unbelievable that it could ever sink away into history.'

'Today we won't talk of what tomorrow may bring.' Nick spoke with a sudden ring of steel in his voice. 'One of the blessings of Venice is that it has none of the torments of road traffic and motor fumes. A few odd smells, perhaps, but nothing damaging to eye or lung. Our gondola is now turning into the Grand Canal, which undulates like a serpent through the city, but one without a sting. I decided at first that we would take *prima colazione* on the *piazetta*, and then I remembered a small place just off the Canal where it is much more secluded.'

'You don't say?' Della gave him what she hoped was a quenching look. 'Is there any place where you have not made love to a woman, Nick?'

'Let me consider.' He lounged against the red cushions and his lean hand trailed the water. 'Ah, I have never done so in a cornfield, where there are too many ears about.'

'Funny man!' She glanced away from his eyes, for there was something about his wickedly amused smile which made her tingle from neck to toe, as if she had been numb for a long time and was just beginning to come alive all through her body. All that she looked at seemed to glow with a vibrancy and a beauty she had never experienced before. All of this was so real and touchable, entering her very being even as she breathed; penetrating her heart and melting those tiny icicles which seemed of late to have grown up like a barricade around her emotions.

Tears filled her eyes and she knew not why, clustering her lashes so the waterside houses quivered like their reflections in the Canal.

'That is the Byzantine church of the Salute.' Nick pointed out the church as they passed it on the Canal, a rotunda dominated by a lovely dome and bell-tower, with groups of stone angels round the base of the dome. 'And to your left, *signorina*, is the Palazzo d'Oro. Is it not a captivating place – all set for romance, or tragedy?'

'The Palace of Gold,' she murmured, and the bronze slates shone like gold as the sun licked across the roof of the house. Beside it ran the stairway streets, the overhanging balconies, and the strings of laundry that in Venice did not detract from the general air of rakish romanticism. It was, she thought, like gliding back into the past when spurred heels had rung upon those cobbles, and gay, laughing women had hung from those casements and plucked a flower from a pot to throw at a dashing young man in a cloak.

A man, she thought, with a face all dark angles and decisive bones, with a smouldering devil in his eyes, and a lean clefted jaw. A man who would have looked not unlike Nick, minus the well-cut modern suit and the tailored brogues. Irresistibly a picture of Nick in a dark cloak, with the hilt of a sword jutting from its folds, sprang into her mind and a smile sprang to her lips.

'Is it a jest for sharing?' Nick drawled quietly.

'Yes, it's quite an innocent one, *signore*. I was picturing you as a Venetian rogue, living in and out of the shadows, and the smiles of gay women.'

'The founder of the family fortunes was a *condottiere*, but of course you had already guessed as much, eh? A *condottiere* in English would be a sort of swashbuckler licensed by his king to plunder for gain and glory, sharing the same with his king in exchange for eventual respectability, a title, an estate, and very likely a wife of good blood. That is how titled families come into existence in most countries, even in yours, Miss Neve.'

'I am sure of it, *signore*,' she said demurely. 'Except that sometimes an exceptional business man or politician will be granted a title in England.'

'And do you know of such a man?' he asked casually. 'A man who has earned his glory by sheer industry instead of merely being born a descendant of a *condottiere*?'

'I might,' she said, airily, her gaze upon the amber and lion-gold façades along the waterfront. 'Venice in days gone by must have been the most intriguing city of the world. Those old palaces look as if they have been witness to many an intrigue. Just look at those secretive courtways and those cypress trees; such places must be haunted.'

'Yes, the *palazzi* of Venice have their ghosts,' he agreed. 'It was a city of poets, martyrs, voyagers, and pirates. Very often must a denouncer have glided up those secretive flights of steps and placed a letter of denunciation in one of those lion-mouthed slots you see in the walls. The Inquisition was in operation in all Catholic countries in those days and this was also a dangerous city to live in.'

'Have you a Venetian background, *signore*?' All at once she felt very curious about him and wanted to know which part of Italy he came from.

'I have a Venetian grandmother,' he said. 'But I was born myself in Tuscany and so I am pulled between the primitive beauty of that land and the mystic appeal of this place. Listen to the bells. They ring at all hours and that is why the thousands of birds are so restless.'

There they flew in enormous flocks above the bell-towers and the spires, the metallic glint of their wings against the blue of the sky. They added to the poetry of the city, and everywhere there were stone drinking cups for them.

'The *angeli santi* of Venice,' said Nick. 'Each Venetian believes that when he dies his soul takes flight and remains in Venice in the shape of a bird. It's a romantic idea and in keeping with the people of this out-of-the-world place. It threw out its web long ago to your English poets and to our Latin lovers – *Venice is there, sitting on the shore like a beautiful woman condemned to die at nightfall.* Always one feels that about her, yet still she fights for life and still she enchants those who come to her.' A small, strange, half-bitter smile twisted at the edge of Nick's mouth. 'Venice is a ravished dream, like love itself.'

Della remained silent when he spoke of love in this brooding way, and she kept her gaze on the stone lion they passed on the edge of a palace landing stage, waiting there in stone grandeur with its left front paw raised upon a stone ball as if to pretend that it might be playful.

Nick, she thought, made pretence that life was a game played to rules that women such as Camilla understood. But today . . . today he returned to Venice in a mood that was not playful. Something had happened here which had made a lasting impression on him . . . Della felt so certain of this that she couldn't bear to look at him in case there was curiosity in her eyes and he mocked her for wanting to know his secret.

She didn't want to know it, she told herself fiercely. She didn't wish to become that inquisitive about Nick Franquila.

The gondolier bent gracefully to his shining *ferro*, the great wooden oar that sent the gondola in a straight graceful line through the water. Erect and well-balanced as a cat the Venetian swung the long black boat around a bend of the Canal and Della glimpsed what looked like a small red palace set among shaggy cypress trees and at once Nick said something to the gondolier and they began to slow down and to glide in the direction of some worn steps with water swirling over the lower ones, leading up to a landing stage.

'This is the Caffe delle Rose where we shall eat,' said Nick, and when the gondola was held still by the *ferro* in the firm hand of the boatman, Della was helped to the steps by Nick and for a moment she felt a strange unsteadiness as she mounted them to the stone jetty. She guessed it was the flickering images of the houses in the water that made her feel wobbly, but by the time Nick mounted the steps to her side she was feeling steady again.

'You were right,' she murmured. 'It does look secluded.'

'And are you unnerved and wishing you had played safe with the other sightseers from the ship?' His hand curved under her elbow and he began to steer her along a lichened path leading to the cypress garden in which stood this *palazzo caffe* of dark-red stone overhung with vines in which grew an abundance of small dark-gold flowers. Gothic windows set within cages of scrolled iron jutted from this mass of greenery and gold. Narrow pointing towers could be glimpsed, and small, hidden patios where birds could be heard, but there seemed no human beings about, no friendly face of a waiter and the white glimmer of a cloth covering a breakfast table.

'The place is closed,' she gasped. 'We can't get breakfast here!'

'We can,' he drawled amusedly. 'This place is run by my cousin Angelo, and though it doesn't open for others until noon, for us it is open at any hour. As you see, it is a small *palazzo*, but such places are not easy to keep in order unless they are put to use, and Angelo is an energetic fellow with a number of accomplishments. He has a chef's diploma, a degree in accountancy, a fine singing voice, and a jovial manner. He has therefore made the Caffe delle Rose an attractive paying proposition without altering its charm in any way.'

'Then you intended to come here from the moment we left the ship?' Della paused under the long leaves of a weeping elm, where a great clump of cyclamen grew wild, and gazed up at Nick with wondering eyes. He was, she decided in that moment, a man who enjoyed playing subtle games with a woman. There were shades of Machiavelli in him, and to love such as he would be like losing oneself in a maze of darkly beautiful trees clipped into fascinating and frightening shapes.

'Perhaps.' He shrugged his grey-clad shoulders and lifted a hand to the cyclamen, a swarthy contrast to the pink flowers. 'I had first to judge your reaction to Venice, but I felt fairly sure that you were not the type to want to sit at a table on the *piazzetta*, sunning yourself in men's admiring glances and sipping iced Cinzano.'

'Thank you, *signore*,' she said drily. 'The women you have known have not been very—' She broke off and bit her lip, for who was she to judge other women when she had left off her engagement ring and pretended she was free to come here like this with an Italian *conte* of *risqué* reputation? A man in whose dark eyes she had once or twice glimpsed a tormented devil?

'Shall you and I come to a small agreement?' he asked dryly. 'If you will forget my other women, then I shall forget your other man – just for today.'

'What do you mean?' Her body tensed and her mind cried a warning. 'What other man?'

'Why, Signor Hartley, of course.' Nick's reply was as smooth as silk. 'What other man would I mean? I have only ever seen you on the ship with the good Joe, and he is old enough to be your father. He is the type of man with whom you feel safe, eh?' With me you feel out of your depth. I make you curious, but I also make you a little afraid.'

'I should hope I wasn't that much of a ninny,' Della scoffed. 'But I do admit that you're subtle and unpredictable – is it really true that this place belongs to your cousin?'

'I invariably tell the truth,' he drawled. 'As matter of fact my Venetian grandmother lives here as well, and after we have had breakfast you might like to meet her. She is a charming old lady, and being fond of music she will enjoy meeting a singer.'

'Oh – you did have all this planned,' Della exclaimed. 'I can't believe that you suddenly decided to come here—'

'I assure you, *signorina*, that my decision was quite sudden.' His hand came down suddenly from the cyclamen and he gripped Della's left shoulder with a sort of restrained anger. 'If you wish to leave without meeting my cousin and my grandmother, then we shall do so. It just seemed to me that your visit to Venice might be enriched if you met two people who spend their lives here.'

'Of course it would!' At once Della was strangely contrite, for all along she had sensed that Venice held a certain memory for him, of bitterness or sadness, and he might not have meant to visit this small family *palazzo* set among the graceful yet rather sad cypress trees. 'I shall be happy to meet your relatives, *signore*.'

'You are sure?' He gazed down at her with those disturbingly dark eyes set in that lean face with the diamond branded on the left cheek-bone. A face that told her – perhaps warned her that there were deep passions within this man, akin to the sea, fathomless, and stormy. 'Do you feel that I am like Aidoneus carrying you away from the sunlight?'

'A little,' she admitted. 'But I shan't worry so long as you let me go again.'

'You want only a day of my time, eh? Poor Proserpina had to endure six months of the dark lord's company.' The sardonic smile slanted across Nick's face. 'I wonder what sort of a woman you would be if you spent six months in my company – *cielo*, don't widen your eyes in that shocked way! I am not asking you to do so, *nina*, though I am sure there would be most pleasant aspects to such a diverting half year. We might both emerge from it – rewarded.'

'Really!' She pulled away from him. 'You speak like an absolute rake, as if you really believe that a relationship between a man and a woman could only last six months before breaking up. Joe Hartley was married for over twenty years and it broke him up when his wife died.'

'The good Joe was lucky to find love,' Nick drawled, leaning back against the trunk of a tree so the leaves played shadows over the lean angles of his face. He plucked a leaf and stroked his lips with it in a mocking way. 'That kind of luck does not come to everyone – perhaps it is the reward for virtue, eh?'

'What a very cynical view to take!' Della reproved. 'Have you been so wicked that you can't envisage real happiness for yourself?'

'What is real happiness?' he asked. 'Have you found it, Della Neve? Do you hide it in your heart instead of showing it in your eyes?'

'What is in my heart is no concern of yours, *signore*.'

'You have your secrets, and I have mine, eh?'

'Exactly.' She shaped her lips to a smile. 'But it's no secret that I *ho fame*, as you Italians say.'

'Poor famished child!' He tossed away the cypress leaf and took her by the hand. 'Then come and be introduced to a luscious *pizza*, cooked as only Angelo can cook them.'

They walked on towards the *palazzo* and Della was acutely aware of Nick's fingers holding her left hand, for had she been wearing Marsh's ring she would not be here right now, breathing the scents of rosemary and the honeysuckle wedded wild to the branches of willow and wistaria. As they came in sight of a side entrance, Della felt a quickening of her heart, as if when they entered this place she would come face to face with a side of Nick which it might be better for her not to see.

It was a large kitchen which they entered, with a red-tiled floor, high white walls, and a ceiling crossed by beams. In a huge dresser there hung gleaming utensils of copper, and along one wall there stretched a range of ovens heated by a glowing charcoal fire. A great scrubbed table dominated the centre of the kitchen, where an array of vegetables had been laid out beside a chopping block. Everything had a spotless, organized look . . . until suddenly a corner door swept open and a swarthy, balding, aproned figure erupted from the depths of the larder with a bag of flour in his arms.

He didn't at first notice the two people who had invaded his kitchen, and when Nick spoke his name, 'Angelo!' he stared with such amazement at his cousin that Della felt instantly sure they had not seen each other for a long time.

'It is you, Nick?' Angelo dropped the bag of flour to the table and a white film spattered the array of peppers, tomatoes, onions and carrots. 'I can hardly believe my eyes – it has been a long time, Niccolo! Years!'

'Six, to be exact, Angelo.'

There was restraint in the air, and Della saw the look of reproach struggling with affection in the dark eyes of Angelo. And then, as if he threw off shackles, he leapt towards Nick and grasped him by the shoulders.

'So good, *mio*! So very good to see you again, and I see you are fit even if you do have the lean and hungry look of a Tuscan wolf!'

Nick grasped Angelo by the shoulders and the laugh he gave had a break in it. 'You look as if you have been enjoying your own cooking, old man. Padroncina has written now and then to tell me how well things have been going and I'm greatly pleased by the success you have made of the Caffe delle Rose.'

'I always said,' Angelo grinned engagingly, 'that there was a commercial side to the family. And you, Niccolo? You have found an occupation of interest and remuneration?'

'I have kept occupied.' Nick's smile was slightly sardonic again as he turned to Della to introduce her to his cousin. 'Anglo, I wish you to meet the Signorina Della Neve, a charming opera star who is a fellow passenger of mine on the ship which has brought me to Venice on this short visit.'

'I am very happy to meet you, *signorina.*' Angelo took her hand and immediately spoke in English as if he guessed from her looks rather than her name that she was from Britain. 'I am a great fan of the opera and go whenever I can spare the time. Have you ever sung in Venice, Miss Neve?'

'No, *signore.*' She could smile easily at Angelo, with none of the restraint which she felt with Nick. 'This is my first visit to Venice, but it must be fascinating to sing here. I have heard that Venetians are great lovers of music, and have fine voices themselves. Needless to say I have sung with Italian tenors in *Bohème* and *Butterfly* and have enjoyed the experience immensely. They have such a natural flair for harmony.'

'You are gracious to say so, *signorina.*' Angelo carried her hand to his lips and kissed her fingers, and she noticed how his gaze dwelt upon her hand as if he wondered if some sort of serious intent lay behind Nick's sudden appearance with a single young woman.

Nick must have noticed that inquisitive glance as well, for he said briskly: 'We are starving for some breakfast, Angelo, and it would be gracious of you if you would whip us up some *pizza*, perhaps with mushrooms, and a jug of your delectable coffee? Even six years cannot make me forget your coffee.'

At Nick's mention of those six years, that long hiatus between his departure from Venice and his return, his cousin gave him a gravely considering look, and Della guessed that he was seeing subtle differences in Nick. Perhaps small lines beside the arresting eyes which had not been there when last they had met. A cynicism in his expression, perhaps. An air of having experienced the world while Angelo had stayed in this tranquil backwater and grown gentle while Nick had become suave, enigmatic, even hard.

With that eloquent look Angelo revealed that his cousin came home to his grandmother's house a different man from the one who had left it. The prodigal who had spent his time and money in the big cities and who now found himself starved of family affection.

'You must both come to the *sala da pranzo*,' smiled Angelo, 'and then I will cook you a big breakfast. I am sure the *signorina* would like to wait in comfort while I clatter the pans and splash the fat.'

The room to which he escorted them was so perfectly Renaissance that Della spent the next ten minutes admiring the Bellini ceiling with its beautifully painted panels, the scrolled Venetian mirrors and chandeliers of ornamental glass. Thick silk ropes held the curtains in huge swags at either side of the long windows, and large Veronese paintings lit the panelled walls with rich colour ... billowing clouds, flame and cloaks and the fiery depths of Italian eyes.

And for the first time Della saw the Franquila crest above the great fireplace, a sculptured gryphon, part eagle and part lion. And there were words in Latin which she could not translate, and she turned with a small inquiring smile to Nick.

'We take and then we guard,' he murmured, and his eyes seemed to look down into hers with personal meaning. 'I expect you have guessed by now that I am the black sheep of this family?'

'Yes,' she said frankly. 'I knew even before I saw you with Angelo that there was nothing tender about you, least of all your mercy. You exemplify the Franquila crest ... you have had to swoop on life, and you guard your independence.'

'By the Virgin,' Nick lounged with a shoulder against the stone carvings of the fireplace, a hand lightly at rest in a pocket of his immaculate linen suit, 'you are just about the most articulate young woman I have ever come across! I take it you would not like to be at the mercy of a man like me? I would not be a good Joe, nor an angelic Angelo, eh?'

She laughed at the very idea. 'You are Nicholas Franquila and unrepentant.'

'A graceless wretch, eh?'

'A wretch, certainly.' She turned to look at one of the paintings, but Nick was imposed upon her mind's eye, assured and direct in his male power, lean and graceful of body, and ruthless at heart. Born that way, or made that way by some incident in his life which had struck deep and made him a dangerous man to be with.

'Nick, what is your birth sign?' she found herself asking.

'Is it necessary for you to know in order to digest your breakfast?'

'I'm merely curious, *signore*, and possibly a bit superstitious.'

'Ah, are there shades of the pagan in the cool-skinned, cool-hearted Della Neve?'

'Those shades are in all of us,' she rejoined. 'I don't pretend to be other than the Dolly Neve who had her name changed.'

'Was your personality changed also?' he asked, and the tone of his voice had changed, the mockery cut out of it by a sudden steely edge.

Della felt that edge, sliding across her nerves, warning her that under his suavity Nick was curious about her, and clever enough to get at her secret if he so wished. She could feel the beating of her heart and this could have been the moment when she revealed the name of Marsh and the fact that he was bound to him by steel-fine, unbreakable bonds. Bonds which forbade her to find another man attractive ... least of all a man to whom women were dolls to be played with.

Yet she didn't speak of Marsh, she escaped again into the forbidden maze where Nick chased her but must never catch her. 'Our birth sign has the most lasting effect on our personality,' she said. 'Or so I believe.'

'And who am I to shatter the beliefs of a nice girl?' he mocked. 'I was born under the sign of Gemini.'

'The heavenly twins,' she said. 'Angel and devil in one.'

'And now you are wondering when I could ever have been an angel.' His laughter was darkly honeyed, his eyes wickedly amused as they swept her face, brushing her features and her skin like a touch. '*Neonata*, you are in some ways still so innocent, but I outgrew my angelic infancy a long time ago. Nick by name, devil by nature. That is the true me and you know it, so don't be fooled because for a day my prodigal soul came home a little hungry to Palazzo delle Rose.'

'I have heard it said, Nick, that a person has to commit a sin before he can dare to be an angel.'

'Meaning that I have committed a sin and you know it?'

'I – I feel it.' She had to avoid his eyes and tossing her straw hat to a chair she went to a wall mirror to tidy her hair. The face reflected there was pensive, its look of youth and purity intensified by the Venetian frame scrolled into the shapes of flowers and tiny gold cupids. The eyes set wide under her winged brows held blue shadows and green danger signals. Her mouth looked as if it quivered . . . as if it hungered. Her own face mader her afraid, for it had such a look of vulnerability. She, the guarded ward of Marsh, was now unguarded in Venice, the city of lost dreams.

'What a wonderful old mirror!' The tautness of her nerves was in her voice, lending to her words a brittle sound. But that was the way she must play it . . . be brittle and gay, as if she were Camilla. Such women amused him, but they also bored him after a while, and she wanted to bore him and be thrown aside by him, carelessly, ruthlessly, as he had thrown aside other women. She wanted his cruelty before she began to want his caress.

'This whole *palazzo* must be filled with museum pieces,' she went on, desperately gay. 'No wonder the tourists like to come and dine under a real Bellini ceiling, surrounded by the works of Italian artists.'

' "We have art in order that we may not perish from life",' Nick quoted. 'It may be better if you remain a work of art, Della Neve, instead of being brought down to earth by the passion of a man.'

'I'd prefer that to the expert kisses of a rake,' she replied. 'I suppose in the absence of your cousin's resource and talent you feel proud of your conquests of women . . . until you become bored. A chef, an artist, or a singer, each has something to show for his efforts, some new thing to create, but women must all seem alike to you after you have charmed them?'

'Are you inviting me to find out if you are different—?' He had just taken a step in her direction when the door was pushed open and Angelo appeared with a laden tray in his hands. At once Nick's look of sardonic threat was lost in a suave smile. 'Ah, breakfast! And what an aroma . . . enough to melt the heart of a devil, eh?'

Angelo shot a quizzical look at Della as he set down the tray on one of the circular tables and began to set out the various dishes of hot golden *pizza*, button mushrooms, thick slices of smoked ham and slices of stuffed egg, dark freshly baked bread, and a dish of steamed asparagus served with melted butter.

'Sit down quickly and eat while everything is nice and hot,' said Angelo. 'I will fetch the coffee and join you in a cup, if I may?'

'Nothing would suit us better, old man.' Nick was still

looking as if butter wouldn't melt in his mouth as he drew out a chair for Della. 'We have much to talk about, and I wish to know if Padroncina is as well as she asserts in her letters.'

'She is well enough for a woman of her age, but,' Angelo spread his hands with Latin expressiveness, 'she misses those who have been part of her life. The old *padrone*, you, Nick, and—'

Angelo broke off, then added: 'I will fetch the coffee, *pronto*.'

When he had left the room, Della proceeded to select food for her plate, and she tried to ignore the sudden awareness of a ghost in that Renaissance room. A drifting touch of coldness, and a whisper of scent. She tried not to shiver, fought not to glance over her shoulder. She had noticed the mass of honeysuckle growing just outside the long windows, but this scent was sharper, more sensuous, as if it came off the skin of a woman.

'You have forgotten to serve yourself with mushrooms,' Nick murmured. 'Don't you like them?'

'Yes – of course,' She picked up the spoon, and then almost dropped it again as the door opened and Angelo came with his silent Latin tread across the thick rug. Della could feel Nick's steady gaze as she helped herself to button mushrooms, and she wondered if he, too, had felt that chilling sense of a third person, far less tangible than his cousin, far less friendly, and gone in hiding again as Angelo poured the coffee and clattered the spoons.

'Padroncina will be so happy to see you, Nick – I have told Margherita not to say a word, so it will be a *buona sorpresa* for her. You remember Margherita, the gardener's little girl with the plaits? She is grown into a very pretty creature, who takes care of our grandmother, and she will become my wife later on in the year, when the busy season is over. We may not seem busy at the moment, but it is still quite early and the diners do not begin to arrive until around noon.'

Nick quirked an eyebrow at his cousin, a fork-stabbed mushroom half-way to his lips. 'You dark dog, Angelo! Why didn't Padroncina tell me of your engagement in one of her letters? Is it a secret?'

'No, but she may have felt that she was reminding you—' Angelo broke off, and Della felt his quick, uncertain glance in her direction, as if he couldn't quite gauge how much or how little she knew about Nick and his affairs.

Trying to look as if she had no interest at all in Nick's love life, Della gave Angelo her warmest smile. 'Congratulations, *signore*. I am sure you will be very happy, for you seem to me a man whose feet are firmly on the ground, and whose heart is big and warm. These are the things most women are looking for when it comes to marriage.'

'You are kind, *signorina*.' Angelo looked rather bashful, whereas Nick gave Della his most nonchalant smile and ate asparagus with the air of a man who cared not a fig for her opinion of him.

'Is Padroncina pleased?' he asked Angelo.

'I think so. She is fond of Margherita and she knows that I need a wife to help me run the *caffe*. I am getting on, Nick. I am forty now, just five years older than you, *mio*. I want a son or two before it is too late.'

Nick wiped his lips with his table napkin, perhaps to hide a slightly ironic twist to them. 'If you are wondering, Angelo, if I am getting similar yearnings, then I can assure you I am not. I do agree that Miss Neve is very lovely, but I don't plan to make her the mother of my son.'

'Indeed not!' Della had never felt so shocked by a remark in her life, for even Marsh had never put into actual words what he mainly hoped for when they became man and wife. To hear the words so flippantly spoken by Nick made her body feel as if it were burning. The look she flung at him was furious, and filled with contempt.

'I shouldn't want *you* for the father of my son,' she said cuttingly. 'You could only pass on your own meretricious attitude towards life and be a bad example to a boy. You had best stay a bachelor, Nick. Marriage is for adults, not for playboys who have to make a conquest of every woman who is reasonably good-looking. It demands loyalty and integrity and I doubt if you possess either of those qualities.'

A small, tense silence followed her outburst, and she knew that Angelo was looking at her with startled eyes. 'Does the *signorina* not know, Nick, that you—'

'Be quiet, Angelo,' Nick ordered. 'Miss Neve is absolutely right about me. I am a rake who has made the world his golden toy to play with. I do have meretricious ideals, and my dreams are all bad ones. You see, cousin, behind that cool and lovely face there ticks a cool British brain. The British keep their emotions in their minds, Angelo; they are not like Italians who have their feelings lower down in their bodies. They evolve from their cold and frigid climate and regard the sun with suspicion. A fascinating race, *mio*, but as difficult to get close to as their national flower – the rose. Reach out and you are stabbed by the thorns that guard the rose from the unwary foreigner. A cruel, unnatural, distant people ... ice to quench the fire of the Latin races. Warriors and writers; lawyers and judges; builders and bankers. But lovers? No! They distrust love and marry not for passion but for a partner to take the strain off living.'

'Do we indeed?' Della looked at him with icy eyes in which burned a blue and angry flame. 'You may be an authority in the art of philandering, but don't set yourself up as a judge of *my* people and their ways. Our loyalty towards any just cause has never been in question – can you as an Italian say as much?'

'No,' he drawled. 'I was but a *bambino* at the time of which you no doubt speak. I don't question British courage or justice. I merely wonder at the way Britannia keeps on producing Puritans like yourself, to whom the mention of passion is like the flick of a whip on the smooth hide of a spirited filly. There could be no roses without their roots in the earth, *nina*. Life is like that, earthy and lusty and cruel. Extra cruel towards those who build for themselves an ice palace in which they hope to live alone, untouched by the hand of a man. A man needs to come along to melt you down!'

'Your conceit must be even greater than I'd imagined if you think I need to be melted by *you*,' she said witheringly.

'You think I could not do it?' He leaned forward across the table and his eyes dominated hers, dark as night yet with a raw little flame burning at their depths. 'I would warn you not to look so chillingly sure of your ice-bound virtue, Dolly Neve. A Latin is not like an Englishman. He is less civilized and therefore less polite when it comes to dealing with puritanical little girls with more wit than wisdom. I think I'd even enjoy melting your icy reserve – those eyes of yours, when angry, are exactly the colour of green sapphires and quite a contrast to your gold hair and your white skin.'

'Save your compliments for your flashy divorcees and your socialites, for they speak your language, Nick, and share your philosophy. They also find it more exciting to take than to give; more fun to be bad than to be good.' So saying Della rose to her feet and flung down her table napkin. 'I can only provide you with a boring day, *signore*, so I had better get a gondola to take me back to the ship.'

'Boring?' Suddenly he sat back in his chair and gave a throaty laugh. 'Is she not amusing, Angelo? The face of an ice-cool angel, the tongue of a virago, and the modesty of a Madonna. She has also, if critical opinion is to be believed, the voice of a pure choirboy, and if such a woman could bore a man, then he would indeed be demanding – or quite dead.'

'You're demanding, Nick, and far from dead.' Another second and Della's sense of humour would have got the better of her, so she turned to Angelo. 'I think I should be going, *signore*. Breakfast was delicious, but your cousin just won't believe that there are women who take cruises for reasons quite unrelated to the hunger to be seduced. I wonder if you will be kind enough to whistle me a passing gondola—'

'Angelo, you will ignore the lady's request,' Nick said smoothly. 'She hasn't the least desire to return to that half-empty ship, to a deck chair and a lonely lunch ... look at her eyes, see how alive and sparkling they are. *Cielo,* they have been opened at last to a little life and danger, and if she dares to run away now – Della, will you dare not to run away?'

'Damn you, Nick!' Her eyes flashed to his dark and mocking face, and she could feel an aching urge to slap that knowing little smile from his mouth. 'Stop trying to pretend that you can read my mind. If you could, then you would know how much I dislike your type. You aren't a nice man, Nicholas Franquila.'

'No, but I'm an honest one.' He rose to his lean and impressive height, and he quirked an eyebrow at Angelo. 'Don't look so concerned, *mio*. The *signorina* and I understand each other far more than she will ever admit, and she knows very well that she is going to stay to meet Padroncina, who does not deserve to be deprived of an interesting visit merely because the visitor disapproves of her guide. That would be too unkind of Miss Neve.'

'Angelo,' said Della in a deliberate voice, 'how did a nice person like you ever come to be related to this offspring of the devil?'

'Our fathers were brothers.' Angelo replied with a smile, but in his eyes there lay a sort of sadness, as if he could recall a time when Nick had been far less cynical, and far more kind in his dealings with people. It was Angelo's look, and her own stab of curiosity, which made Della change her mind about leaving the *palazzo* before she had met the grandmother of the two cousins. Nick wouldn't have stopped her, she told herself, if she had really wanted to leave.

'Nick hasn't twisted my arm, Angelo,' she said. 'I should like to meet your grandmother very much.'

'*Bene!*' Angelo's smile lost its anxiety and he gestured at the table. 'You have had enough to eat, *signorina*?' You would not like more coffee?'

'*Grazie, no*. It was all very nice and satisfying.'

'What of you, Nick?'

'I am replete, *mio*. It was a good meal, and you will wish to get the table cleared. Will Nonna be ready to receive us?' Nick shot a look at his wristwatch. 'She does not spend the morning in bed, does she? It feels strange that I no longer know her routine, and I can remember how she used to be up early, caring for her garden. But she is older by six years—'

'Yes, cousin.' Angelo picked up the coffee pot and ran his fingers over the warm, silver surface. 'Six years can be a long time to the young, and the old. The young develop, but the old start to fade. I am glad for Nonna that you came to see her. She will be in her chair on the patio lending out from her rooms – shall I go and tell her you are here?'

'No.' Nick's brows were drawn in thought as he stood in a shaft of sunlight through the windows, so that Della noticed the intermittent gleam of silver in his black hair, and the fine, deep etching of his lips as he brooded there, shot through by a memory, perhaps, of the days when he had been younger, happier. Oh, God, he could make her spit fire, yet all at once she felt a clutch of sympathy for him. He had not been born so careless of the feelings of others, so something had happened here in Venice to make him the way he was. There had been some traumatic wound to his feelings ... something he could not forget, or forgive.

'No, *mio*,' there seemed to be an edge of pain to his voice, 'I should like to give Nonna a surprise – if her heart is strong enough to stand seeing me without a warning?'

'She is frail,' said Angelo, 'and that will be a shock for you, but her heart is sound enough for her years. Sound, but sad, you understand me? Sad that you have kept away so long, for you were always her favourite grandson.'

'Devil that I am?' Nick murmured, and abruptly he reached for Della's hand and clasped it almost hurtfully. 'Come, *nina*, let us go and see the only woman who truly loves me.'

CHAPTER FIVE

DELLA heard the cool sound of a fountain and saw a wild tangle of honeysuckle at the arched entrance of *la nonna*'s patio. As she and Nick entered this little courtyard, a gem of weathered stone and shrubs banked into soft clouds of colour, Della saw the small Psyche just inside the archway, her wings scarred by the sun and the rain, and she had a sudden sense of magic, of stepping out of the world of anxious realities into a quiet place where love had been, and where love still lingered, watched over by the little goddess of the heart. There was a fragrance of herbs and also a scent of lemons, and Della gave a sigh of delight as she saw the lemon trees with their fruits ripening from green to gold on the branches. And in the shade of the trees stood a white cane chair, the high fan back of it framing the head and shoulders of the woman whom Nick called Padroncina . . . the little mistress.

Draped around that small figure was a black silk shawl, so deeply fringed that it almost reached the ground, and to the right of her, seated on some steps, was a girl in a bright dress, her dark hair bound in a silky plait around her hair. On her lap there was a blue bowl into which she was shelling peas, and as her hands worked among the green pods there came the flash of a ring.

Suddenly she lifted her glance and smiled at the woman in the cane chair, but neither of them had yet noticed the couple who stood as if entranced in the shadow of the archway. Della thought what a perfect picture the girl and the woman made, seated there in the Italian sunlight, one of them with dreams of love in her smile, and the other with a lifetime of memories in her eyes.

Della was about to whisper her thought to Nick when all at once she felt the bruising grip of his fingers about her wrist, tightening until she believed her bones would be crushed.

'Nick!' His name broke from her. 'You're hurting me!'

The girl across the patio caught the sound of her voice and she swiftly turned her head to look at them. Her eyes were dark and startled in her healthy young face, made pretty by the carnation flush beneath her olive-tinted skin. Her lips formed an oval of surprise, and her chin was rounded above a smooth throat adorned by a cross on a chain.

The instant Nick saw the girl his fingers relaxed their hold on Della and the relief from pain was swiftly followed by the realization that Nick had relived a tormenting vision when he had first seen the girl with his grandmother.

He had thought he was seeing a ghost . . . the same one who had drifted into the dining *salone* for a few chilling seconds.

'Signor Conte?' The fingers of the girl's left hand clenched the crucifix, almost as if she was seeking protection against him.

'Margherita?' He quirked an eyebrow, and Della knew from the caressing drawl in his voice that he was again in command of himself. 'But of course – Angelo told us you had grown up to become a beautiful young woman.'

And so saying he began to saunter towards the girl, and the silent, darkly shawled figure of his grandmother. Della could feel herself holding her breath, for there was a quality of drama to this meeting after such a long time. Nick had grown into a man of the world, while *la nonna* had grown old in her quiet garden. Six cynical years had marked the face of this handsome grandson. Six long years had brought both of them closer to hell and heaven, the silence broken only by the cool splash of the fountain and the twittering of birds. A flame-winged butterfly flew to a flower and a petal fell, and then Nick was at the chair of his grandmother, and on his knees like a courtier, his hands holding hers until his dark head slowly bent and he buried his face in the frail, veined hands.

It was true to say that never in her life before had Della been so moved by the action of another human being, and it was extra startling that it should be Nick Franquila who brought such a lump into her throat and made her feel so unbearably an intruder into a very private moment.

She looked about her, rather wildly, and then she heard the sound of bells chiming somewhere among the denser trees of the garden, and she followed the sound on impulse and soon came in sight of a small chapel set among the cypress trees. It had the perfection of old and weathered things, so alone and still except for its bells. Vines twisted their way to its roof and curtained the walls with their green foliage, and the door stood partly open, as if inviting Della to come inside. She hesitated, for she had left her hat inside the *palazzo*, and then she remembered that she had a chiffon scarf in her bag and she drew it out and draped it over her hair. Then she entered the chapel and walked along the aisle to the altar, where there stood a Madonna of blue and gold, and where an amber-coloured candle had been lit and was burning softly in the tinted light falling from the peaked windows.

Della knelt and closed her eyes and for several minutes she prayed for the strength she had not reckoned on when she had sailed away from England. She had been anxious about her voice, but had not felt that she would never recover her skill, and her will to sing.

It was her meeting with Nick which had made her feel the need to pray.

'Oh, Marsh,' she whispered, 'you should have come

with me . . . you should, for once, have put me before your business deals. I – I needed you, but you said that all I needed was a rest and plenty of sea air. You were so sure of me, so certain that I could never be anything but your devoted slave. But, Marsh, if you give a slave a taste of freedom she is likely to let it go to her head . . . or perhaps to her heart.'

Della sighed and let her gaze rest on the serene face of the Madonna on her pedestal. She knew how much she owed to Marsh, so that his trust in her loyalty, and in her love, should never for a second have been shaken. But her very existence felt shaken, and as her gaze drifted to the altar in this Italian chapel she could no longer face calmly the thought of herself as bride to Marsh. She had grown up knowing it would happen, yet here she was trembling at the picture which the little altar evoked . . . herself in white brocade, standing beside Marsh as they exchanged the vows that would bind her to him body and soul. Never before had she asked herself if she loved him enough to marry him, for he had always been so good to her. She had never thought of their relationship as a sort of bondage, for he had carried her away from the wreckage of her parents' car and he had shaped for her an entirely new life. Without Marsh she would have been placed in a home for orphans, for neither of her parents had possessed any close relations, the sort who would have been willing to take into their keeping a homeless child of ten. But Marsh had taken her into his home, and into his heart.

Despite all his deep involvement in big business, Della knew that Marsh cared for her. He was not a man to speak of what went on in his heart, but Della knew in her own heart that no man did so much for a woman unless he admired her, and desired her, and wanted her to complete his life for him.

With a little groan Della covered her face with her

hands . . . there should be none of these doubts in her heart, for Marsh was everything a girl dreamed of. Tall and fine-looking, generous to a fault, clever and cultured, strong yet capable of tenderness.

He was a wonderful person, yet here she was with her pulses beating out the name of another man . . . here she was with the dark and cynical features of an admitted rake superimposed upon the face of her fiancé.

It was all wrong, and she couldn't excuse the fascination which she felt by saying it had happened because Marsh had guarded her too well. He had made it possible for her to have a career and she had sung on the opera stage with dark and handsome Italian tenors.

So what was it about Nick Franquila that haunted her? He possessed none of the qualities which she admired in a man, yet he seemed more real, more deeply disturbing than anyone else she had ever known.

Oh, God! No! Her heart couldn't have been so foolish as to let *him* into it!

She rose and fled from the chapel as if suddenly her thought were a blasphemy, and there among the cypress trees stood the man who had shaken the ground under her feet. He was smoking a cheroot with laconic ease and for several minutes he just lounged there looking at her, watching her as she removed the square of chiffon from her hair and put it away in her bag.

'I hope,' he said at last, 'that you now feel composed enough to come and meet my grandmother? Come, she is waiting to know you.'

'Can anyone ever really know another person?' she asked. 'I don't think we really know ourselves.'

'A few veils are a mercy,' he drawled. 'A total confrontation with another human soul might be too terrible to endure. It is best not to look beyond the face, *nina*.'

'When did that become your philosophy, Nick? I don't think you were born a cynic, or a sinner.'

'No more than you were born an angel,' he rejoined. 'The sacrificial sort who must deny herself in order to please someone else.'

'W-what an odd sort of remark, *signore*.' Panic clutched at her heart, for it was becoming plainer all the time that Nick knew more about her than she actually knew about him, but how had he acquired his knowledge? Her path had never crossed his before, and she couldn't believe that he read the opera reviews. Even so he would not have learned of her engagement, for that had been a well-kept secret between Marsh and herself. Marsh was not a man to encourage gossip about his private life and he had not released to the Press the news that Della was to marry him.

Was Nick being clever and making an inspired guess about her private life?

Her blue-green eyes swept his sardonic face and tried to read there an answer to her troubled question.

'Why is it so odd?' he asked. 'From the very beginning you have emanated that sort of aura. "Touch me not, for I have taken vows." There are two kinds of vows which women take—'

'You take liberties,' she flashed. 'If you're allowed to. I just don't wish to be another scalp on your belt, *signore*. You surely have a big enough collection without adding my hair.'

'Such wonderful hair,' he drawled, and his eyes dwelt upon the thick, sun-shot fairness of her hair as she stood there in the sunlight shafting through a break in the trees. 'But as you said once before you don't want my well-used compliments, so come and talk to Nonna who has never been anything but sincere and true to herself.'

'Doesn't it trouble you, Nick, that you have disappointed her hopes in you?'

'Love makes allowances for our toes of clay.' He held back a branch so Della could pass him on the path that led back to *la nonna*'s patio, and for an instant his gaze caught and held hers. 'There is no perfect love, and it isn't love at all unless it holds forgiveness for our sins. If you don't know that, Dolly Neve, then you have never known love.'

'I wouldn't call you an authority on – on spiritual love.' Della slid past him with all the caution of a cat with its fur on end. 'You know of only one kind of love!'

Instantly his eyes were dangerous, and instantly she knew that she had spoken too soon and had not put enough space between them. His left hand moved with serpent speed and his fingers had hold of her nape under the thick gold of her hair, and when she gave a little cry he smiled, ever so slightly, with lips that swiftly stilled any further sound she might have made. Lips warm and hard, pressing upon her a kiss that ripped open the heavens and made a storm there among the trees.

Marsh had kissed her, but not like this. Marsh had held her, but never with such bruising arms.

'No—' She wrenched aside from Nick's mouth and felt his lips like a knife across her throat. 'Don't – please!'

'You asked for this,' he whispered roughly. 'You scorned me as a sinner, little saint, so I will make you sin with me, here where the trees hide us—'

'Nick – don't!' She was desperate because she knew he meant his threat. 'We've enough to regret without—'

'Enough?' His laughter soft-stroked her with mockery. 'Not nearly enough, *mia bella*. Life is for living not for crushing like a rose between the pages of a prayer book. Beauty is for the man who dares to take it, not for the puritan who puts it in a glass case like a French clock.'

It was that touch of humour from him which broke the tension and made her laugh shakily. 'You devil, Nick! Bad as you are, you wouldn't seduce a woman in your grandmother's garden. Well, you've had your fun and frightened me, so now let me go—'

'Did I only frighten you?' He looked down into her eyes, searching them, she knew, for her confession that for a few wild seconds something had flared between them and made them the only living realities to each other. A purely physical response, Della was fiercely sure of that. Nick could not be denied his masculine appeal to any woman's senses, especially here in this Italian garden where the cypress trees made a secret embrace easy to hide. She had to forget, blot from her very being that moment when everything had been so incandescent in his arms. She had to make her eyes deny that it had happened and she gave him back a cool and dispassionate look.

'Did you hope you were going to melt me down into one of those adoring heaps of womanhood you are so used to, Nick? Did you kiss me to try and break my pride? It's what you like, isn't it? To see a woman grovelling in the net of your charm . . . I wonder, *signore*, who hurt you so much that you have to keep taking your revenge on other women?'

Della had not meant to go so far, but now the words were spoken and couldn't be recalled. For an instant his face was totally still, like a mask of bronze, and then his eyes came alive in the mask and they glittered with such a terrible anger that he might have struck her if there had not been a sudden diversion in the shape of Margherita. She appeared among the trees in her bright dress, saying in a bright and innocent voice:

'Padroncina has sent me to look for you both. She grows anxious, *signore*, and fears you will go away again—'

'I am not going away just yet, nor is Miss Neve.' In a flash the anger was covered up by a smile and only Della knew how close he had been to an eruption of frightening temper. 'We are coming now, so lead the way, Margherita.'

The path was narrow and they walked single file until

they reached the patio, and all the time Della could feel Nick behind her, tall and lithe, and with his reined-in temper like a whip across her shoulders, so that it was a sheer relief when they came in sight of his grandmother's chair. Immediately the little woman flung out a hand to him and there was in the gesture a loving demand and the lonely appeal of someone who had waited for him a long time and despaired of his return. Now she wanted him within touch of her hand, and he hastened over to her, his hand under Della's flinching elbow.

'I had trouble locating our guest, *carina.* She went astray among the trees after a visit to the chapel.' His fingers nipped Della's elbow as if warning her that she must be nice to his grandmother, the only woman in his life who fundamentally mattered. The only woman he cared about hurting, as he had hurt her by staying away so long.

'Miss Neve, I wish you to meet my dear *nonna*, the Signora Isalita Monittoro-Lanzi. Nonna, this young English lady is Della Neve, who is a star of the opera. She is taking a cruise on the same ship as I, and she had a wish to see something of Venice.'

'How do you do, *signora*?' Della held out a hand to Nick's grandmother, and was aware as they shook hands of the shrewd Italian eyes taking in her every feature.

'I am very well, Signorina Neve, and happy to meet a friend of my grandson's. You are, if I may say so, very slender to be a singer in opera. Do you much like it?'

Della was startled by the question, for it was the first time anyone had ever asked such a thing. Everyone took it for granted that it was an unadulterated pleasure to sing almost without pause in a long, involved story of passion and intrigue. No one ever questioned the strain, or wondered why her recordings of lighter songs such as those from *The Merry Widow* had such a wider appeal. She had never dared to question her own joy in light comedy songs, and her lesser joy in operatic arias . . . she had always felt that it would be disloyalty to Marsh and his belief in her talents.

Yet here . . . here in Venice, at her very first meeting with an elderly woman who did not get about to see much of the world any more, she had been asked a very shrewd question and in her heart she knew the answer. She hungered to sing always the gay, light, romantic songs, and her voice had gone temperamental on her because she hadn't the courage to tell Marsh that she didn't wish to sign for another opera season. He merely thought she was tired and in need of a holiday, but Della knew that it went deeper than that. With the help of experts he had moulded her into an opera star, but at heart she was a singer of the people – a girl of the people – and Nick's grandmother knew it.

A smile lit up Della's eyes, and her eyes lit her face, with all its innate charm and intelligence, and its pure fire in the shape of her lips and her cheekbones. The Celt in her was suddenly in evidence, for her mother had come from the High Pennines, the land of the long winter and the beautiful summer.

'Nick, will you go into my *sala* and fetch chairs,' his grandmother commanded. 'Also ring the bell and that sweet child Rita will bring us some wine. She is still shy with you, Nick. You always had the effect of making girls run from you, or to you. But she is good for Angelo. They are nicely matched, for they are two nice people.'

'You never did think me as nice as Angelo, did you, Nonna?' Nick bent a quizzical smile upon his grandmother, while his lean hand caressed the fringe of her silk shawl. 'Miss Neve will probably endorse your opinion, for she thinks me a wicked rake.'

With these words he went into the *palazzo* by way of the steps and the arched entrance into his grandmother's suite. His sardonic words hung in the air between the two women, and then *la nonna* gave an amused chuckle.

'Is this what you really think, Miss Neve, that my Niccolo is a wicked wretch who breaks hearts?'

'I – I really don't know him well enough to pass an opinion, *signora.*' Della hoped she didn't sound too much of a humbug, for she knew full well that she had summed up Nick at her first sight of him. 'We only met on the ship and had our own small circle of shipboard friends until he asked me if I'd like him to show Venice to me. He said he knew it well as members of his family were Venetian.'

'Then why should Niccolo insinuate that you think him a man not quite nice to know?' The Signora Isalita gave Della an old-fashioned look, as if she knew very well why a young, cool-skinned English woman should find her darkly distinguished grandson a man to keep at arm's length . . . if she could manage to do so.

'In some ways he's too dangerously nice,' Della smiled. 'His charm conceals the fact that he takes few people seriously, that for all his acquaintances he is a lone wolf at heart.'

'So you have formed an opinion of him, for all that you deny it, *signorina.*' *La nonna* nodded her head, as if this was only to be expected. 'Yes, he goes out of a room and it is like salt forgotten at the table. Such personality is a gift or a drawback, for it attracts many people and among them at times the wrong sort.'

The old lady brooded a moment after she made this pronouncement, and Della studied her without being too obvious about it. Her skin was sun-dark ivory, lined all over as ivory is when aged. Her eyes were as raven dark as Nick's, and she was a woman lovely with age and wisdom, and the fragility of fine bones. A heart of diamonds glittered like huge tears against the lace collar of her dress, and she was both indomitable and a little sad, Della thought. As though she had come sadly to terms with the fact that Nick would never stay long in Venice any more, and that her life would steal away as the days stole away into the dusk.

'Yes,' she murmured, almost as if she were talking to herself, 'there is an unpredictable streak in the Latin male, and I suppose the Latin woman learns to live with it. But to an English woman it would seem like stepping on to unsteady ground when she is so used to the stability and calm temperament of the Englishman. Yes, you come of a race so different from ours that it is like crossing a snowflake with a sunbeam. The snowflake can only melt, or flee in terror from a total loss of herself. You would not like that, eh, Miss Neve?'

'Indeed not!' For a brief moment, even as Della made her quick retort, there flashed into her mind that sheer, incandescent merging with Nick during that embrace among the cypress trees; that rapturous release of the senses, so primitive and pagan that she had known she was with a man who could destroy her if he so wished and throw her carelessly aside when her destruction was complete.

Nick was now more dangerous than he had been before that kiss . . . he could be as loved as he could be hated, and Della knew that her salvation lay in hating him.

To love Nick was to come face to face with the devil in his soul.

'Italian men, my child, do not suffer from the European male's dislike of sentiment. The Italian appreciates the exciting difference between men and women, but this balance of good sense is upset by a devilish, passionate vendetta should a woman ever be the root cause of a tragedy in a Latin male's life.' *La nonna* leaned a little forward and her gaze took and held Della's. 'Nick will return at any moment, and what I am going to tell you, I am going to tell quickly. Perhaps because it hurts me to see him misunderstood, for in my heart I have a deep *amorevolezza* for this strayed grandson. You see, when he was your age he was husband to a girl whom his father, the previous Conte, chose for him when he and the girl were still in the schoolroom. I knew the marriage would be a disaster because I knew Niccolo to have in him the fire and the freedom of the Venetian, for his mother was my daughter. I knew he should have been left free to choose his own bride, but his father the Conte was an arrogant, self-willed man determined to bring an heiress into the family rather than a happy, loved-for-herself girl. Donaleza was half-Spanish and the family she came from was a highly strung one, with a history of melancholia.

'Within a year of the marriage a child came, a little girl whom Niccolo adored as he could not adore his wife, who wavered perilously between gaiety and melancholy. She was mystical at times and fond of spiritual subjects. She claimed that dreams were a kind of astral journey more real than life itself. She had a striking beauty which could look beaten and tragic at times, so that people thought Nick was unkind to her, which he was not! She was like a flame, shimmering hot or cold, and not only self-destructive but dangerous to those who were near to her – Nick and their small daughter, Trini. From the beginning of the marriage a shadow seemed to lay over it, and a normal person felt always troubled in Donaleza's presence, for she was like Ellida, the lady from the sea. Then the father of Niccolo passed away and he thought it wise to bring Leza, as he called her, to Venice for a while, to my *palazzo* here in this tranquil garden. They came one late afternoon, just as the sun was setting over the waterways and burning on the cobbles of the courtyards so they seemed to glow like living coals. Venice is always strangely beautiful and a little tragic as the sun goes down, and Niccolo realizes now, to his eternal regret, that he should never have brought his strange wife in sight of

Venice, with all its water, all its bridges, all its memories of martyrs and carnivals.

'Nick has a penetrating pain which lingers, Miss Neve, for it was here in Venice that Donaleza threw their baby daughter from a window of a *casa* on the canal, the home of a friend of ours to which they had gone to tea. Why she did it we shall never know, but I am in no doubt that the ears of my grandson are shells, forever holding the scream of his child as she plunged down into the water, to choke there before he could reach her and save her small life. Donaleza they took away to a hospital for the insane, and it is a strange fact, Miss Neve, that while she lived, and she lived for six years in that state of half-living, my Niccolo was the essence of kindness to her. It was only afterwards, after the gondola hearse had taken her dead body to the Isola Cipresso, the dark coffin smothered in a mass of white frangipani, the flower of the dead, that he suffered a sort of delayed shock of terrible anger and distress. He left Venice, went far away from Italy, and he did not return until two hours ago, when he came with you.'

In the silence which followed this awful and shocking revelation about Nick, a lizard palpitated like a living, torn-out heart on the sun-struck steps, and the sadness was sculptured even deeper into the lines of *la nonna*'s face. Across the patio came the soft splash of water against stone, like tears that kept on falling for the dead baby, and the destroyed heart of Nicholas Franquila.

Nothing ... not a thing in the world could ever recompense him for that small quenched life he had loved. Never again would love be anything but an unbearable pain for him, so that each time love showed the tip of its flame he snuffed it out with cruel fingers and lit fickle passion and cynical sin in its place.

Who could blame him ... who could truly condemn?

'You will say nothing to him of what I have told you,' said his grandmother quietly. 'It is just that I wanted you to know, for you seem different from those women he allows himself to be photographed with in the magazines. Rita buys for me these magazines and I read about him – the handsome playboy *conte* whom these women try so hard to marry. *Per Dio!* As if my Niccolo will ever marry again! These women, they are nothing! A carnival he follows so the noise will stop him from thinking too much of what has spoiled his life. He plays, yes, but love has no more meaning for him, for love was torn too cruelly from his heart and in its place there is a stone. You understand, *signorina*? You are *simpatica* towards him now I tell you of this sadness he has lived with all these years? Trini would now be a lovely girl of thirteen, for she was much like Niccolo, with great dark eyes and the dent in her chin. My great-grandchild—'

La nonna shook a sad head, while Della felt the pain and the sympathy flood her heart and fill her eyes with tears. Tears which she blinked away fiercely as she caught the sound of his deep voice from the *sala* and knew him to be returning, Margherita at his side with the wine carafe and the wine glasses on a tray. Nick carried a chair and as he came down the steps the smoke of a cheroot, clamped between his teeth, drifted upwards to veil the expression in his eyes.

The proud lift to his head, the strength and tension of his jaw, told Della that he would not favour a revelation of his secret, so it rested with Della to act with such normality that he wouldn't guess that she had been told about his tragic marriage.

Strange that she had never associated Nick with a wife ... a mistress, yes, or a sweetheart of his youth who had played with his affections. But the story which *la nonna* had revealed was terrible and more deeply scarring than a love affair could have been. A shudder ran all through

Della as she visualized Nick's shocking despair and anguish when he had carried his baby daughter out of the canal, so still and waxen, like a pretty doll, the great dark eyes closed for ever, never to sparkle again with life and love of the tall man who was her father.

Perhaps Nick felt the tremor that shook Della, for as he set down the chair he looked into her eyes and his look was ironical. 'Do relax, Miss Neve, and sit here while we drink a glass of wine with Nonna.' And then he smiled with all the devastating charm of which he was capable. 'It must be a long time since a woman of such Botticelli fairness sat in this old courtyard, and to celebrate the occasion I have chosen a wine called Angel's Tears for us to enjoy. And you, Nonna, what have you to say of our guest?'

'She is a charming young woman, Niccolo, and sensible. *Mia,*' his grandmother turned to Margherita, 'do fetch Angelo so we might all celebrate this occasion. It is a long time since we were all together.'

'*Si*, Nonna.' Margherita placed the tray on the patio table and smiled shyly at Nick. 'Angelo will be busy in the kitchen, but he will spare the time to come and drink a glass of wine.'

The young Italian girl hurried away in the direction of the kitchen, and *la nonna* shot a look at Nick, as if she wished that he, too, had someone so unspoiled and kind-hearted to love him. 'Angelo has been lucky, eh? Rita will make him a good wife.'

'It is only what Angelo deserves, Nonna.' Nick spoke with not a hint of irony in his voice. 'Come, sit down, Miss Neve, then I can rest my legs by sitting on the steps. Ah, it is quite a day! The sun shines and the birds sing, and you look well, my grandmother. Often I have thought of you sitting here under the lemon trees, with that magnolia grandiflora growing over there, the great stone pots spilling their jasmine, which you planted when

I was a boy. And up there the golden rays flaming through a sky an Italian master might have painted. There is no place on earth quite like Italy, especially for the exile.'

'Must you,' his grandmother leaned forward and took hold of his hand, 'must you remain an exile, Niccolo? I am sure the house and estate at Tuscany need you, for no matter how good is a manager, he is not the master with a love of the place in his bones. What can America give you, except a bad name with the women?'

'Really?' He quirked an eyebrow at her, and then with a careless smile he raised her hand to his lips and kissed her fingers. 'I find some things to do which do not involve the woman, believe me. Well, *carina*, do you believe me?'

'No,' his grandmother rejoined. 'I read the other day of your association with an American oil heiress, and she tells the reporters you are to become engaged. This is true, or false, Niccolo?'

'Take a guess,' he said dryly.

'I think there is a devil in you.' She lightly slapped his cheek. 'How did you persuade a nice girl like Miss Neve to spend the day with you? I hope you are not planning her seduction?'

'Nonna, what a thing to say in front of such a nice girl!' He flicked a look at Della, who joined in the game and gave him a cool and haughty look. 'Miss Neve would slap my face in no uncertain manner if I tried my tricks on her. No, she is strictly a career girl and takes life very seriously. She has little time for games, and even less time for the people who play them. Is this not so, *signorina*?'

'Without a certain amount of dedication no career can hope to succeed, *signore*. As you know, I'm only taking this sea cruise in order to rest my voice.'

'Does that mean you will not sing for us, Miss Neve? Ah, but I had been looking forward to hearing you,' said Nick's grandmother. 'I am fond of music and used to play the piano when I was younger.'

'Nonna is modest,' said Nick. 'She was a concert pianist before her marriage, but when she became the wife of a high-placed Venetian diplomat she had to give it up and play only on social occasions, or for her family. As a boy I loved nothing better than to sit beside her on the piano bench while she played to me the music of Liszt, Chopin and Schumann, and Nonna actually taught me musical composition. But it was Angelo who had the gift for singing, and I am sure he could bring tears to even your eyes, Miss Neve, with his rendering of an old Caruso song, *Because*. You may not know it—?'

'But I do,' she said, 'and I love it!'

'You are not a classical purist, then?' He quirked an eyebrow at her. 'The singers of opera are not always as broad-minded as the great Caruso was known to be. He loved melody for the sake of melody, and personally speaking I find some aspects of opera rather hard to take. It often sounds like a verbal battle between the leading soprano and the leading tenor. Or am I being blasphemous about your art?'

'No, *signore*. I am merely surprised that you should take an interest in it.'

'But I'm an Italian,' he drawled. 'I have an ear for music, or did you imagine that all my finer instincts were, blunted by my shocking life?'

'I – I suppose I imagined you were too sophisticated to enjoy the pleasure of music – t-to really enjoy it, I mean.' That unwavering look of his, with mockery flickering in it, was hard for her to endure. It made her voice trip, and it made her heart thump in her breast, for a terrible truth lay at the heart of his way of life, and she had grown afraid of letting pity show in her eyes. 'For every authentic music lover, there are those who pretend to like it for the sake of fashionable first nights at the opera. They gush all over the singers and send flowers, but it's too often the people up in the balcony who really love and appreciate a certain aria or a duet. It is they who wait in the cold and the rain to hear us sing, and I confess, *signore*, that I sing to them rather than the beautifully dressed patron in the boxes and the stalls.'

'An admirable confession, *signorina*, and one I applaud. You know,' a smile stole into his eyes, 'it was a mistake to change your name from Dolly, for at heart you remain a girl and you only pose as the cool lady which the name Della imposes on you. Ah, here comes my good cousin to join us for a glass of wine! Angelo, old chap, I hope you don't mind that we drag you away from your culinary works of art in order to drink to the return of the prodigal?'

'Not at all, Nick. I am – delighted to see you, and the minestrone will be happy in the pot until I return to it.'

'You will be good enough to pour the wine, Angelo,' said his grandmother. 'You have such a steady hand to match your heart, *mio*.'

'You are kind to say so, Nonna.' He bent a smile upon her, yet Della had the feeling that Angelo was disturbed by Nick's visit, and she noticed that Margherita had stationed herself in the citrusy shade of a lemon tree and her eyes were fixed not upon her fiancé but upon the face of Nick, as if she were dazzled by his rakish good looks and his history, which she would be aware of as she had lived at the *palazzo* since she was a child. Was Angelo feeling the traditional jealousy of the steady man of the family who had stayed at home and never strayed from the path of duty? Was he afraid that Nick would turn the pretty head of Margherita and make him seem unexciting by comparison, someone whom life had not scarred with tragedy, as it had scarred Nick. The pale gold wine was poured. The stemmed glasses were handed round, and instinctively all eyes dwelt on Nonna.

'So I must speak the toast because I am an old woman

to whom the years have brought a little wisdom.' She looked steadily at Angelo, and then let her glance travel to Nick. 'I have two grandsons whom I love dearly, and today, when my old bones feel as if the sun is no longer as warm as it used to be, my grandsons are here with me. Angelo, *mi amore*, you will have contentment because you have earned it. Rita, you will share that contentment, and let me tell you, child, that it is the gold in the ring even if it isn't the diamond.' Nonna paused, as if to let these words sink into the mind of Margherita, then she turned to look at Della, and in her dark eyes, still so alert in their network of lines, there was a shadow of regret.

'You, Miss Neve, are like the memory of mimosa on a southern wall, for some women can only be a memory and never a reality. I shall think of you when you have left Italy. I shall remember you, but first let me say this. Sing the music which you love, or the music will not wish to be sung at all. Do you understand me?'

'Yes—' It was strange, but Della felt in that moment that she could have broken into song and not felt the awful constriction of her throat, as if hands were gripping her and stifling her will to sing. 'Yes, *signora*, I think I do understand.'

'Good.' The dark eyes smiled a moment, and then *la nonna* was looking again at Nick, whose lips were quirked in an enigmatic smile as he stood waiting for his grandmother to pronounce his fate.

But all she did was to raise her glass to him, and all she said was that she hoped he would return again to the Palazzo delle Rose before she passed on to Nirvana.

'Nonna, *cara*, you will live a hundred years and more.' He carried his wine glass to his lips. 'I drink to your health, and to thinking of you always here on this patio. *Ciao!*'

'Ciao!'

All of them echoed Nick and they finished their wine . . . but there were no tears, only a whispered blessing, when he took his leave of his grandmother. From the *sala* there drifted the sound of music, for Margherita had gone in quietly, no longer looking at Nick, and had placed a record on the player.

'Schumann,' said Nick, his fingers firmly under Della's elbow as he guided her to the jetty alongside the water, where a small party of tourists were just landing so they were able to hire the gondola the four laughing people had just left. Nick glanced back once . . . the trees looked black as he and Della stood there by the water's edge. In the tall, black-flame shadows of them grew tall crimson foxgloves. Suddenly his fingers were clenching hers, as if pain shot through him, and she glanced down at the bronzed darkness of his hand against her pale skin, and she saw the knuckles standing out whitely.

The last thing Della saw in the false twilight of the *palazzo* garden was the fan of a bird's tail moving on a branch as the bird hesitated between staying and flying away. Then abruptly, with a flutter of its wings, it hopped the branch and was gone.

'Come,' said Nick, and he helped Della into the gondola, and the water rippled like silver scales as the great oar thrust into it and the graceful black boat glided away from the sea wall of the Palazzo delle Rose.

CHAPTER SIX

DELLA spent the remainder of the day in Nick's company, but from the moment they were steered away from the *palazzo* his entire manner underwent a change. He became a polite, distantly charming, instructive guide, and he ensured that she didn't miss any of the tourist attractions which Venice had to offer.

They strolled the inner court of the Doge's Palace, where the helmeted god Mars and stern-faced Neptune stood in marble grandeur at the head of the Giant's Stairway. And as they walked, she and Nick, through the cool and cloistered courts, she didn't mind that he was reserved with her and didn't speak again of his family. Somehow his mask of polite charm suited her own mood, and when they stood beneath a statue or a painting and he talked of it, she saw the brooding power of his face and knew him to be a man of unimaginable depths. The dark mystery and dusky gold of the Byzantine churches made her very aware of the darkness of the soul through which Nick had passed. The candle flames reflected in his dark eyes, but his thoughts were impenetrable and he talked only of the history, the antique romance and intrigue of all that they saw together.

They watched the two stone Moors strike with a hammer the huge bronze bell high above the Campanile, and they went to eat lunch at a small *trattoria* above the hollow lap of water on a rough platform of stone.

They enjoyed *fritto misto*, a mixed dish of fried shrimps, scampi, soft-shell crabs and sardines. It was delicious, and followed by *petti di pollo*, breasts of chicken with tiny green peas and potatoes. Nick insisted that she have dessert or his Italian sense of hospitality would not be satisfied, and so she had a succulent lemon pancake and a cup of creamy coffee.

For a while at lunch Nick's manner had relaxed, and as he leaned back against the rough sea wall of the café he smiled at the fabulous skyline of Venice and for an instant his face lost its closed-in look of reserve, and deep secret pain.

'Venice is heart-shaped seen from the air,' he remarked, lighting a cheroot and puffing the smoke into the clear, blue air.

Della didn't question his remark, and a little later they made their way to the Corte della Seta, the colourful court of silks, where Della found herself unable to resist a lovely length of wood-violet silk that would make up into an attractive dress. Nick wanted to pay for it, but she said firmly that she wanted the fun of buying her own keepsakes of Venice.

'Where can I buy a Venetian goblet?' she asked him. 'I want something really nice . . . for a friend.'

'I think I know of a shop.' He escorted her through a busy little market-place, where she saw fruit arranged in colourful mounds, all sorts of fish laid out on large green leaves, many kinds of cheese, and huge rough-skinned melons. The shop was tucked away behind tiny windows, a small treasure trove of glass and copperware, and antique costume jewellery. With Nick's help Della finally settled on a Murano goblet that seemed alive with beauty in her hand, amber-coloured, delicately shaped and so transparent that it had to be packed most carefully in yards of tissue paper and a cardboard box lined with straw.

They were about to leave the shop when Nick suddenly paused to admire an antique bracelet of Florentine design. He bought the bracelet and dropped it into the pocket of his jacket, and Della supposed that it was intended as a gift for a woman he knew.

They made their way back to the campanile, an animated sea of marble, warmed by all the people who passed beneath its arcades and stood in groups beneath the stone angels and gargoyles that decorated the towering walls. Across the wide pavement of the *piazzetta* there strutted the many pigeons, in and out of the legs of the people, plumaged and cooing. A couple of nuns in wide coifs ushered their brood of convent pupils in and out of the arcades and galleries,where there were sculptures and carvings both religious and warlike.

Della was happy to wander away the day with Nick, and to listen with great interest as he talked of Venice. Whatever his intimate memories of the place, he kept them well banked down, a glimpse of slumbering fires she only now and then caught sight of in his eyes.

They talked of Desdemona, for her legend was still very much alive in Venice, where long ago the Moors had gilded palaces and golden-haired Venetian brides. Those had been the days of gay regattas on the Grand Canal, with a parade of the courtesans, and masked saturnalia. And it could all be imagined as Della stood with Nick on the balcony of the lantern-tower high above the *piazzetta*, to which they had been swept in a lift. Below them clustered the gilded domes and the red-tiled roofs, speared by the narrow church spires. The day was so clear that to the north they could glimpse the glittering peaks of the Alps.

It was an unforgettable view of the city, laced with canals that looked jade green from this height. A fabulous city of two hundred marble palaces and a thousand bridges. A city of bells and birds, and churches with such fascinating names as that of the Barefooted Friars.

'Venice is always a remarkable place,' Nick said, leaning there against the balcony of the tower. 'It has a way of conquering the most hardened heart, and its *leitmotiv* is the sadness of great beauty in decay. In storm, with lightning rippling over the water and threatening the domes and towers, it thrills the nerves like a scene from *Othello*. Like a certain woman, Venice is a place that the heart remembers. She lacks the earthy richness of Rome, the hilly splendour of Tuscany, and the velvety charm of Florence – instead she has a mysterious magic of her very own. She has a soul!'

And up there on the tower Della shared the magical experience of sunset over Venice, the *capolavoro* as it was called. As the red-gold sun sank away into the distant lagoon, the sky slowly filled with a translucent shade of green and the domes and spires seemed softly outlined with sheerest gold.

Twilight stole over the city and the lights of the waterside houses began to glitter and gleam in the canals. Far off in the distance the decks of their liner were outlined by her lights, and then the sound of her siren floated across the water, like the call of Cassandra.

'Time now to go.' Her hand was taken by Nick and they entered the lift and were quickly swept as if from heaven to earth again. But he didn't lead her on to one of the motor-boats which other passengers were taking. In his crisp Venetian he hailed one of the lovely lagoon craft, on the bows of which were painted flowers and symbols. The sails spread themselves above the boat and these, too, were patterned with stars and signs of the Zodiac.

'These lagoon craft are called *bragozzi*,' said Nick, as he took the seat at her side. 'You should not say good-bye to Venice in a motor-boat.'

She smiled but didn't speak, for her voice might have betrayed how moved she felt as they sailed across the *laguna* instead of cutting too swiftly through the water to the side of the great ship. She felt the fascination and mystery of the Venetian night, for modern dress was concealed by the shadows and Nick might have been wearing the tunic and hose of days gone by, and she might have been clad in velvet edged with sable.

Then, to add to the magic, the man who guided the boat began to sing in a dark rich tenor voice. *Maridite, maridite, donzella. Che donna maridada, e sempre bella.*

Della had often sung in Italian, so she understood the words, and she kept her profile turned away from Nick and pretended to be absorbed by the stars trapped in the dark jade sea. Get married, get married, girl, the married woman is always beautiful! Della was grateful for the breeze, for it cooled her cheeks. Did the boatman suppose that she and Nick were sweethearts? She felt the crazy beating of her heart . . . and when they mounted to the deck of the *Gothic Star* there was still no respite for her disturbed emotions. Before letting her go to her stateroom, Nick said quietly:

'You must accept from me, Della, a keepsake of our day in Venice.' And he took hold of her wrist and clasped around it the Florentine bracelet which she had believed was meant for some other woman.

'Nick . . .'

Her protest was swiftly silenced by the pressure of a finger over her lips. 'Wear it in memory of Venice, and because it becomes you.'

An hour later she still wore it as she stood by a porthole in her stateroom, clad in her robe and unable to bring herself to dress for dinner. She wanted to hold on to the memory of her day with Nick, and as she gazed from the porthole and saw the lights of the ship reflected on the water she felt a reluctance to join the other passengers. They would be laughing and talking of their tour of Venice, but her own had been too deeply impressive for light discussion.

Today had been one of the most memorable days of her life; she even felt that her life had been altered in the most subtle way by what she had learned, and experienced, during her visit to the *palazzo* which was haunted for Nick by the strange girl he had been coerced into marrying by his father.

No wonder his grandmother had said with such sad firmness that he would never be able to face the thought of marriage ever again. His first had been too traumatic and always he would carry in his heart and his nerves the agony of that moment when his adored little daughter had screamed ... perhaps crying out for her papa.

In an instinctive gesture of horror, as if she had actually witnessed the cruelty and tragedy of that scene in Venice, Della threw her hands over her eyes and the gold bracelet, engraved with Medici motifs, fell heavily against the bones of her wrist ... as shocking, almost, as if a hand reached out to clasp her by the arm.

'Oh, Nick! 'she gasped, and she knew why she couldn't face the thought of dinner. Nick would be at the adjoining table with Camilla, and she would see him as a stranger once more, his gay and reckless mask back in place, hiding the man he truly was from the eyes of the gay and reckless people whom he had chosen to keep noisy and bright the carnival that kept the memories at bay.

Della sighed and bit her lip so hard that she almost drew blood ... the evening ahead had to be faced so she might as well get it over and done with, and bracing her slim shoulders she walked to the built-in wardrobe and opened it. She studied the dresses inside and decided that she must attempt to join Nick's carnival ... the dress she selected to wear was of pure silk organza in blue and green, with romantically extravagant sleeves and a deep décolleté back. As she put it on she recalled the first time she had worn the dress which looked so puritan until she turned about and her bare back was revealed. Marsh had been rather shocked by the dress, and when they had danced he had seemed uncomfortable, and as if he disliked touching her bare skin in such a public place as a supper club.

Nick, she felt convinced, would be amused by the dress.

Before leaving her stateroom Della took a long, impersonal look at herself in the full-length mirror. The turquoise material had a soft glow against her skin, and she wore her hair in a fair, silky pageboy style. She looked chic and outwardly composed, but she didn't dare to look too closely into her own eyes. Tonight they were more green than blue, as if shadowed by a hint of storm.

Her little clock chimed and her nerves tightened at the sound. The time had come for her to go to the restaurant deck and to walk into the dining-room as if her day in Venice had been as carefree as that of the other passengers who had gone ashore.

As she mounted the stairs the tannoy music was playing ... *be still, my foolish heart.* Della caught her breath and her fingertips traced the enamelled motifs of the bracelet she wore, her only adornment, her only piece of jewellery, lending its antique lustre to her very modern dress.

Foolish, indeed, had grown her heart ... her compassion let loose for the young man who had left the strong, hard body of Nicholas Franquila a dozen years ago.

To her intense relief Joe Hartley was about to enter the dining-room as she turned into the corridor. 'Della!' He waited for her, looking big and solid in his dinner-suit. 'Good evening, lass, and may I say how stunning you're looking?'

'Thank you. You're looking distinguished yourself, Joe.' She put on her gayest smile and tucked her hand into the crook of his arm as they walked together into the dining-room. The music was still playing above the chatter, and even as Della made her light responses to Joe's remarks, with all her nerves she was aware of the song ... that foolish, sentimental song she had once sung at a charity concert ... *there's a line between love and fascination ... love and fascination.*

Joe pulled out a chair for her and she sank down into it. She said good evening to the honeymoon couple ... oh, yes, Venice had been perfect, just wonderful, and filled with history. Yes, wasn't San Marco a place all set for romance ... no, they had not lunched on the *piazzetta* but had chosen a little *trattoria* jutting above the water ... with water-plants crusting its walls like a coat of golden mail.

'That must have been nice for you and Mr. Hartley,' said the girl, in all innocence.

'I didn't ...' Della broke off and bit her lip as female laughter trilled out from an adjoining table.

'Sure, it was fun.' Joe pressed his hand upon Della's and looked her straight in the eye, letting her know that he understood, and that he was prepared to stand like a shield between her and the man who was amusing Camilla ... perhaps with a droll résumé of his guided tour of Venice in the company of the English girl.

Della felt certain that her face went very white ... when life had been cruel to a man, and the cause had been a woman, there was no reason why he shouldn't be cruel in his turn. Camilla laughed again, and Della didn't object when Joe ordered a couple of gin-and-tonics. She needed the drink and when it arrived she drank most of it without pause.

All through dinner she kept her back to Nick's table; she didn't glance once in his direction, and was resolved never again to lower her guard and allow compassion to blind her to what the years had made of him. She must never forget again that all true feeling had been struck as dark and dead as lightning striking a tree and burning all that made it grow upright and fine. Only the body and bone of Nick was left, and in place of emotion there was mockery. She almost wished that his grandmother had not revealed what lay in his past, for it hurt, more than it would have done, to know that he sought to be hated because he was afraid to be loved.

'Champagne, waiter,' she heard Joe say. 'The four of us are going to have a party.'

And that's exactly what they had, Joe insisting that the honeymoon couple join them afterwards in the ballroom, where for all his bulk Joe turned out to be quite a dancer, and where he managed to get hold of some rolls of streamers and several bags of confetti and had everyone joining in the party. The noise and gaiety and stamping went on until almost midnight, when Della had a sudden sense of claustrophobia in the overcrowded ballroom and had to seek a breath of fresh air and a little solitude.

She slipped away while Joe was caught in the Kissing Ring and sought the seclusion of an upper deck, where she leaned gratefully against the cool rail and gazed at the sea, darkly scalding mass of starlight, with the wake writhing after the ship like a great, white-mottled snake. Here on the aft-deck all sounds were muted, and there was hardly a breath of wind so Della didn't feel cold as she rested her elbows on the rail and let the marvel of the night soothe away her emotional aches and hurts.

'Some daemon calmed the air, and smoothed the deep.' What demon? she wondered. It surely took an angel to make all this beauty. Demons made only torment . . . Lucifer fallen from heaven to walk the earth with feet of fire.

Della tautened as she caught the sound of footfalls on the quiet deck . . . let it be Joe, she prayed, but as the footsteps came nearer, with a sort of relentless precision, she knew who it was who had tracked her to this secluded corner of the ship. She also realized that her figure in the sea-coloured dress was outlined by the sea-light and she must have the look of a gilded moth trapped in the strands of a web. The entire surface of her skin seemed to prickle with fear of the man who came out of the night like a spider claiming its victim. Fool ... fool that she was to have left the safety of the ballroom and the security of Joe's protection.

A gasp ... or was it a groan ... escaped her as warm hands came down on her cool shoulders, bared by the deep plunging backline of her dress. 'I very much like the exquisite state of your undress,' Nick drawled. 'All through dinner I had the pleasure of seeing your back turned to me, and there is such an elegant mobility to your shoulderblades.' And quite deliberately, as his words died away, he bent his head and she felt his lips against the bare skin of her shoulder, lingering and drifting down over the flinching blade-bone.

'How dare you ...?' She clamped her teeth, furiously angry with him for coming to her like this, straight from Camilla. 'Why can't you leave me alone?'

'No woman who wants truly to be alone comes to stand in the starlight, she goes and hides in a much less romantic place.' Abruptly his hands tightened on her shoulders and he swung her to face him; his fingers gripped her filmy sleeves, and her eyes were so frightened, like pools of quicksilver, for her foolish heart had led her to this moment and her heart was mocking her as much as he did.

'Leave me alone, Nick. I'm waiting for Joe!'

'The good Joe, eh? With whom you always feel safe and secure as if he were a father.' His hand slid down her left arm and his fingers found the Florentine bracelet. 'I think if you truly disliked me, Della, you would not wear this. What is it, I wonder? Do you fear that friendship with me would be like heaven trapped in the arms of hell? You know, after our day together, it was most ungracious of you to ignore me at dinner, and I refuse to believe that you find Joe so fascinating that you cannot take your eyes from him.'

'I like Joe very much, and we've been over this ground before, Nick. Because I spent an agreeable day with you, being shown the attractions of Venice, that doesn't mean I have to make cow's eyes at you across the dining-room. Besides, you had company, and from the sound of her merriment I can only assume that you were amusing her with anecdotes of our tour of Venice.'

'Do you really believe such a thing?' His slanting eyes suddenly lost their sensuous quality and narrowed, raking her pale skin, her turquoise dress, and the blaze of golden hair about her upraised face. '*Cielo*, what a despicable opinion you must have of me, to think I would use you as an object of ridicule. Don't you know what kind of a woman Camilla is? She laughs to flatter a man and makes pretend that his every word is a gem of wit. *Per Dio!* I made no mention of our day together, and what it meant to me to be able to see Venice again in sympathetic company, but may I ask you if you made a joke of it all with *your* table companion?'

'Nick, how can you ask . . .?'

'How can you accuse?' He flung her away from him, against the rails, and his features were etched into a mask of furious contempt. 'Women are all alike, the consummate Janus with two faces. All day the smiling face of sweet charity, but with the fall of night the features change to those of sweet corruption. Look at the dress you are half-wearing! You deserve to be spanked . . . or are you really asking to be seduced?'

Della clung to the rails and felt the band of the Florentine bracelet pressing into her wrist, reminding her of the moment when he had given it to her. Now it seemed to burn her arm and she began to wrench at the clasp with fingers that shook. 'Y-you can take this back – give it to Camilla – she's the one who wants to be seduced by you.'

'Keep it,' he snarled, 'or throw it overboard. Yes, throw it into the sea, which rarely gives back what it takes.' He swung on his heel with these words and strode off in the direction of the stairway. Della held the unclasped bracelet in her hand and his words made her eyes close tightly in pain and self-reproach.

What had come over her? She had never been cruel in her life, yet something drove her to say hurtful things to Nick, who had already been hurt beyond healing. Tears welled and scalded her eyelids. Why was she so on the defensive with him ... and then as if afraid to face the answer which the sea might whisper, and the stars might spell out, Della left the deck and made her way to her stateroom. She was in no mood to return to the ballroom and suddenly felt indescribably tired, as if all the events of the day had become a burden which she could no longer endure.

She undressed and went to bed, and nature was kind enough to pull a gentle blanket over her troubled mind and she slept undisturbed until the morning.

The ship would cruise about today, giving her passengers a chance to enjoy the brilliant sunshine, which was flooding in through the porthole near Della's bed and banishing last night's shadows. She was soon out of bed and under the shower, and at the touch of the water she felt a sudden desire to take a swim before breakfast. Swiftly she towelled herself and slipped into a jade-green swimsuit and a short terry jacket, and because her hair was the fine sort that disliked getting wet she kept on the rubber-petalled hat in which she had showered and left her stateroom in the hope that she would find the swimming-pool empty at this time in the morning.

To her delight this was so and she quickly threw her jacket over a nearby rail, kicked off her sandals and dived into the clear green water of the pool. It was heavenly, and because swimming was one of the ways in which she kept fit as a singer she was very proficient in the water and after a few laps across the pool she hauled herself up the steps and made for the diving-board. She was standing there, arms poised, her slim body dripping with water, when a lean figure came half-naked through one of the archways and, fingers pinching his nostrils, jumped with a sort of animal abandon into the water.

Della stood as if pertified on the board, still poised for her dive, when the man's head and shoulders popped out of the pool and he saw her standing there, outlined by the sunlit sky. Their eyes met and held and seemed unable to withdraw from that collision of the dark eyes, lashes water-tangled, and the turquoise gaze bright with shock. It was so unfair, she thought. She had chosen this early hour to swim alone, and it was just like cynical fate to keep throwing her into the path of this man.

Setting her chin, she dived and splashed water in his face. The mask of the clown had to be assumed if she was to survive this strange infatuation for a man who could never have a permanent place in her life. Did it not happen time and time again to a person taking a cruise in warm and romantic waters? Someone with a special kind of aura stood out in the crowd and made the trip dangerously exciting . . . she just had to accept this and not make a drama of it each time Nick swam into her orbit.

'Good morning, *signore*.' She silently prayed that he would agree to forget the way they had parted last night. 'I had no idea you were such an early riser. Doesn't the water feel good?'

'Ravishing,' he agreed, and in his eyes there glinted a sardonic little signal of a truce, if she so wished it. 'I had no idea you could dive like a champion. Can you swim equally well?'

'If you are challenging me to a race, then you are on.'

She struck out gracefully for the far end of the pool and felt the surge of the water as Nick thrust his lean, tanned body into pursuit of her. A thrill of excitement lent speed to her body ... it was like having a tiger-shark at her heels and she could feel the panic tingling in her bones as she sensed him catching up with her, until suddenly he dived and came up through the water ahead of her and deliberately trapped her in his sinewy arms.

'Nick!' She wriggled like a captured eel and his wet face was all creased with mocking laughter as he gripped her wet body close to his.

'It has been a rule of mine for a long time never to let a woman get the better of me, so I rarely play fair.' His shameless face came close to hers and he kissed her in the water ... it was a most curious, almost shocking sensation to feel her limbs all tangled up with his and her lips caught in protest by his lips. They were like mingled currents of light and dark ... swaying water-plants locked together for endless moments ... sanity overcome by a misty chaos of the mind and the senses.

Play fair ... Nick could never play fair, but she must. She must, for her own sake and Marsh's.

She raised her hand and yanked at Nick's black hair until he yelped and set her free. Immediately she struck out for the side of the pool and hauled herself out of his reach and there she sat on the tiles in a wet, breathless heap and saw with relief that other people were arriving to share the pool.

Her hands now felt shaky as she tugged off her cap and let her hair tumble about her flushed face. She was filled with a sense of shame and betrayal, for if she had never left off Marsh's ring she would never have become involved with Nick ... so involved that she fought with him as she had never fought with Marsh, and felt unbearably shaken by his kiss.

'All that exercise has made me feel ravenous.' Della

jumped to her feet. 'I'm off to get some breakfast.' She made for the rail where she had flung her terry jacket and left her sandals, circling the pool and aware of Nick cutting his way through the water with a brown gleam of limbs and body. He hauled himself out of the pool just as Della slid her feet into her sandals, and she cast him a look through a wing of her hair, defying him to come closer, her eyes bright with warning that she would not be touched again.

He stood there tall and dark against the green reflection of the pool and drops of water tangled in the crisp hair of his chest and ran down over the skin of his shoulders. The sun slanted into his eyes and he shielded them by lowering the lids and letting the thick darkness of his lashes take the glare. The entire look of him disturbed Della, not faintly but fiercely, and she snatched up her jacket and quickly covered her body, in the wet clinging suit, from the dark sweep of his eyes.

'Will you allow me to join you for breakfast?' he asked, somewhat dryly, as if he knew most of what was going through her mind. 'I promise to be on my best behaviour, and will have it brought to the sun-deck if you would like to have breakfast there?'

'I – I don't know, Nick.' She drew the edges of her jacket together and kept her gaze fixed on the small medallion that glinted against the brown, shaggy strength of his chest. 'You make promises, but you have no conscience about breaking them. It isn't fair – I want to be friends, but you make it far easier for us to be – enemies.'

'Enemies?' he said softly. 'I don't think of us in that way, but then you are English and I am Italian and very possibly we place very different interpretations upon the behaviour of a man with a woman. Let us agree to be perplexed by each other, for it will ensure that we shall not become bored with each other.'

'I think it's safer with you, Nick, to be a bore. You then leave well alone.'

'Is that what you really want, Della?' He quirked an eyebrow. 'For me to leave you alone? It could certainly be arranged, for I permit no woman to become so essential to my day, or my night, that I cannot see the sun or the moon unless it is shining in her eyes. Shall I go away?'

It should have been easy to say yes, for he admitted that he was only amusing himself with her. The word was there on her lips, her release from this dangerous association, yet other words, spoken by an old sad woman in a cypress garden, made it too hard for Della to deny him his amusement of her – at breakfast, at least.

'I'm a fool to give in to you, Nick,' she said. 'I know I can't trust you, but neither can I resist breakfast on the sun-deck. Can you really arrange it? The waiters don't like their routine upset as a rule.'

'Rules were made to be broken.' Nick smiled with his lips, but his eyes had an inscrutable look behind the shield of his Italian lashes. An almost ruthless look, Della realized, as if he never allowed his desires to be frustrated. Her heartbeats could be felt like tiny warning drums as she looked at him . . . would he have his way with her before this voyage ended?

'I – I'll dash and change into dry clothes,' she said. 'Order bacon and eggs for me. I shan't be long.'

'At your service, *signorina*.' His voice and his glance were rampant with amused irony, and Della had to control her impulse to dash away from the look in his eyes. It was a look that beckoned, and a look that followed her as she left him with all the composure she could muster. It was a look that gave her pause at the office of the Purser, where she signed for her jade and diamond ring. The time had come to replace it on her hand . . . her talisman against the effect which the Conte Nicholas di Fiori

Franquila was having on her feelings. Her safeguard against this man who was more dangerously attractive than any man had the right to be . . . a sleek and tawny-pelted tiger with a thorn buried in him, which he would allow no one to remove.

When Della appeared on the sun-deck she was wearing a daffodil-coloured dress, as crisp and bright as the sunlight. Her hair was looped back in a jade pin, her lips were softly painted, and on her left hand she wore Marsh's ring.

Nick was waiting for her, tall in narrow-fitting dark cords and a silk shirt thrown open in the heat, very white against the tanned skin of his throat. He looked absolutely male, indolent in the sun and yet simmering with vitality. Below the rail where he stood the sea was a great wing of green veined with waving silver lines.

'You do indeed look like the memory of mimosa on a southern wall,' he said to her. 'The waiter is bringing our food on trays and will not be more than a few minutes. In the meantime come and look at the sea, which is the exact colour of a dragonfly.'

She came to his side and very deliberately she raised her left hand and rested it on the top rail. In a flash the sun had become imprisoned in the jade and had caught fire in the guard of diamonds. Della stood very still and gazed at the sea, but inwardly her nerves were tied up in knots and she could not control her slight jump when Nick spoke.

'Very pretty.' He touched the ring with the tip of his forefinger. 'Why have I not seen it before? Is its sudden appearance supposed to have some deep significance?'

She flushed and suddenly felt how inadequate she was when it came to putting Nick in his place. In an instant he had the advantage of her and made her feel that she had played a childish game with him.

'The ring is worth rather a lot of money,' she was on

the defensive and couldn't be otherwise, for she was guilty of playing a game of deceit. 'I'm afraid when I swim or play deck games that I shall lose it.'

'We were not swimming or playing games yesterday,' he drawled. 'Or am I wrong and we were play-acting?'

'I no more than you,' she rejoined, her hand clenching the rail while the gems sparkled and gleamed in the sunshine. 'Are you so entirely frank with people that you can afford to judge me, Nick? Did we not say at the start of the voyage that we were both entitled to our secrets?'

'And today is your day for revealing your secret, eh? Why, because I kissed you in the pool and made you feel entirely like a woman for the first time in your life?'

'That's a typically arrogant assumption of every man, that his kiss is the open sesame to paradise.' Della could feel herself trembling with temper and anguish. 'I want to be friends with you, Nick, but if you're going to lash at me–'

'Our waiter comes with our breakfast,' he broke in smoothly. 'Do control your tears, *nina*, or he will suppose that I have been brutal to you, and you look incapable of being anything but lovely and innocent yourself. Would you add to my terrible reputation?'

'I – I don't believe any more in your terrible reputation,' she said quietly, and she went to her chair and took her breakfast tray from the waiter, who had carried both trays to the sun-deck with the dexterity of his calling. He smiled at Della, bowed at Nick, and left them to eat for a while in silence.

'Nick . . .' Della had to speak and attempt some sort of an explanation. 'I want you to know that I left off my ring for a reason that had nothing to do with you. The man I'm going to marry is the finest man any girl could have the good fortune to know. He has looked after me since I was a child and taught me everything I know. But when I came aboard the *Gothic Star* I felt like someone who had always been sheltered and had never known what it was really like to face life without the protection of – of my fiancé. I took off my ring on impulse. It was silly of me, but I wanted to find out if I could face up to certain situations on my own, without this ring as evidence that I have only to say my fiancé's name and there's nothing that need worry me; nothing I have to go without. I – I suppose I wanted to be as anonymous as possible, and no woman can be that with such a valuable ring on her hand.'

'The fiancé is rich, then? Well-known and important?' Nick leaned back in his deck chair with his cup of coffee and his gaze was as polite and impersonal as if they had just met. 'And he is older than you, of course, if he has cared for you since you were a child.'

'He's not in his dotage,' she swiftly defended Marsh. 'He's one of those men with the brains and will to succeed fairly early in life, and he isn't much older than you, Nick. He took charge of me when I lost my parents—'

'And you feel you owe him an eternal debt of gratitude?'

'No! I love Marsh with all my heart! I – I can't imagine life without him—'

'Marsh Graham?' The name was spoken with a sudden clipped accent that made Nick seem suddenly very foreign, and formal. 'He is the man you are going to marry?'

Della should not have felt so startled, for Marsh was, in his own way, as newsworthy a figure as Nick. His business activities were widely reported; it was in his personal life that he was reticent. 'I see you have heard of him, Nick.' She sipped at her coffee and tried to appear composed.

'Who has not heard of one of England's foremost tycoons?' The note of irony was back in Nick's voice. 'So it was he who changed your name from the warmth of Dolly to that of the cool and perfect Della? I understand that he has a famous collection of jade and Asian filigree work, so I take it you will be joining them?'

'You can take it, or leave it.' Again he had sparked off her temper and anything might have been said in that moment if there had not come shrilling from the direction of the children's play-pool the sudden sound of a child's frightened scream. This was followed by an instant of silence, and then the shattering of china as Nick's tray was hurled from his knees as he leapt to his feet and went racing in the direction of the pool.

With shaking hands Della set aside her own tray and followed his tall, imperative figure. Even as Della ran along the deck a riot of thoughts were running through her mind. A child had screamed, and for Nick the clock had sped backwards and everything was forgotten but the one small soul he had loved . . . and lost.

A cluster of scared children were at the edge of the pool, and Della saw Nick hurl off his shoes and jump into the water, and when she reached the poolside he had brought a child to the surface of the water, small and limp, with honey-coloured hair trailing wet and limp over his arm. He struck out with his free arm for the ladder of the pool and Della helped him to lift the little girl out of the water on to the tiles.

'There, Honey, it's all over – all over.' Della held the sobbing child as Nick massaged the water out of her lungs. Some of the other children were crying and the frightened attendant had appeared. Nick, his face pale and drawn under his tan, shot a fierce look at the young woman who was supposed to keep an eye on her charges at all times.

'Where were you?' he demanded. 'This child could have drowned and you would have been responsible!'

'I – I only turned my back for a moment – these things happen so quickly—' The girl bit her lip and looked as if she would burst into tears herself.

'You deserve to be reported,' Nick said cuttingly. 'You women amuse me, with your pretence of care and love for children. All you think about is yourselves! Your minds are filled with self, self, self!'

'Nick,' Della touched his wet shoulder and felt the tenseness in his body. 'Accidents do happen so quickly—'

'Honey was chasing her ball,' a small boy tugged at Della's hand. 'She slipped, I saw her, and fell in the water.'

'You see, Nick.'

He stroked Honey's hair, and only Della knew that for a few tortured minutes he had lived through the death of his daughter Trini. 'Are you now feeling better, *neonata*?' he murmured, his voice a husky caress as he spoke to the child in his arms.

Honey buried her face against his chest, and Della knew that never again would she think of Nick as a man without a heart.

CHAPTER SEVEN

DELLA saw no more of Nick until the evening of that fraught day. She was in her stateroom when a young officer brought a letter to her from the Captain. It requested that she join him and a few other passengers for cocktails in the Blue Lounge, and because on board ship such a request was almost a royal command, Della decided that she had better attend and wear something rather special.

In fact she welcomed the invitation, for all day she had felt on edge. After lunch, at which Nick had not appeared, she had gone along to ask the ship's doctor if Honey was all right. 'Most children bounce back from these experiences like resilient rubber balls,' he had reassured her. 'She'll be as right as rain after a good sleep – I do wish, however, that all mothers would have their children taught how to swim.'

'I believe Honey is rather afraid of the water – it seems strange, Doctor, that the things we fear should have a way of pouncing on us.'

'It's just life and its odd little quirks.' His shrewd eyes had studied her rather pale, tense face. 'You saw the incident, eh? Would you like a sedative to help you rest awhile? It is upsetting to see a child in distress.'

'I'm all right, Doctor, now that I know Honey is safe and sound.' She had smiled and hurried away, and after sending Honey a box of sweets and a jigsaw puzzle, she had spent the afternoon in the smoke-room, where a few people played cards while others snoozed. Della had read one of the detective novels which Marsh had given her, along with the white roses which had slowly faded and shed their petals.

The roses had now been taken away and in their place stood flame-coloured gladioli in a vase. Della had not asked the steward who had sent them, and he had seemed to take it for granted that she knew. They stood tall and proud on the dressing-table as she prepared for the Captain's cocktail party, and she closed her mind to why Nick had chosen that particular shade of flower. She forced herself not to think, but the words seemed written across the mirror when she looked into it, and they danced like imps as she moved her hands to arrange her hair and her ring flashed and gleamed.

There was no forgetting what he had said to her ... that in his arms she had come alive as a woman for the first time in her life. There was no denying the physical pleasure of that embrace in the water, but it had not involved her heart, only her body. Long ago she had given her heart to Marsh, who was so strong and so firmly set on his path through life. Once she became his wife, his strength would become hers and never again would he be weakened by someone like Nick.

She would be able to feel compassion without this frightening pull on her emotions. She would be able to look at a worldly rake of a man without the fear of being fascinated by him, for fascination was mostly based on the curiosity of a girl who had her virtue still intact.

Suddenly, as she fastened the gown she had chosen to wear, she felt a great need of Marsh and longed to hear his deep and reassuring English voice. Tomorrow the ship put in at Naples and she would go ashore alone – yes, all alone, and she would arrange to put through a call to Marsh and hear him say he was missing her and needing her. Such reassurance would make all the difference and give her the strength to withstand the subtle assaults which Nick was making upon her. She meant nothing to him, no woman did, or ever could, and so all he had in mind was a seduction that would reduce her to the level of other women who had fallen victims to his dark, fateful attraction. Women whom he used to revenge himself against Donaleza. Women who started by loving him and ended by hating him.

She didn't want to love Nick, nor did she wish to hate him. She wanted to reach out to Marsh, for he was her guardian against the dark fears of the night. He was her life, and she could never take to him a heart and a body another man had used. He was a perfectionist who had fashioned her to suit his own perfect taste . . . the gown which she wore at this precise moment had been chosen by him and there wasn't a line to it that didn't suit her, not a shading of colour that didn't blend with her cool, fair looks.

It was an entrancing peacock-green velvet dress, very simple in design so the richness of the material could be seen to perfect advantage against her clear skin. The dress flowed supple and regal down over her slender body, and she thought how lost and tiny was young Dolly Neve in that poised figure reflected in the mirror.

She fastened her jade necklace, stroked perfume over her skin, and assured herself that her Greek chignon was smooth and secure. If she was strikingly attractive tonight she didn't really notice; her awareness was centred on the fact that Marsh had selected her dress, running his firm strong fingers down over the velvet and smiling his approval with lips that sternly controlled any other emotions he might have felt. It wasn't out of mere flippancy that he was called 'face of stone' by his employees, and Della knew that she was possibly the only person in his life who was ever allowed to see him truly relaxed. In front of other people he was always a figure of command; she alone held the key to his inner personality. To the person who needed her no longer as a charming ward and companion, but as a wife.

Her fingers clenched the jades, for at the start of this

sea trip she had turned from him like a child resenting authority. But now she girded herself in the expensive armour of the dress he had bought her, and armed herself with his jades . . . the magic stones, radiating protection against the dark powers that lay smouldering in the eyes of a dark man.

Beware the dark stranger, she thought, as she locked the door of her stateroom and walked to the staircase that led to the deck on which the Blue Lounge was situated.

As she mounted the stairs she heard the whirring of the ship's stabilizers and realized that they had sailed into rather rough waters. The brilliance of the day had given way to a sulky sunset; a sky of choked-pink clouds, smoky and shot through by streaks of flame – somehow expressive of the storm within herself. There were black waves riding the sea, and she gave a slight shiver and glanced away from them, and was glad when she reached the doors of the lounge and pushed them open to enter.

Several of the guests were already assembled, officers in white dress uniforms, men in white tuxedos against which the dresses of the women looked vivid and gay. There was a clink of glasses, a sound of laughter punctuated by a sudden silence as Della entered the room. At once she knew herself the focus of all eyes, taking in the perfection of her dress, the fairness of her hair, and the almost defiant brilliance of her eyes. She saw one of the women slowly arch an eyebrow and she knew what the woman was saying to herself . . . that it was just like an opera *diva* to come to a cocktail party dressed to kill. Della tilted her chin and braved all the eyes that were fastened upon her.

'Miss Neve!' The Captain came across to her, resplendent in his dress uniform. 'How gracious of you to attend our soirée, and may I say that you look very beautiful?'

She smiled and accepted his arm. 'I have heard it said,

Captain, that sailors are the champions among flatterers. I suppose in contrast to all that churning sea any woman would look fetching.'

'My dear Miss Neve, you are not any woman.' He smiled down at her, iron-grey head firmly set on broad shoulders and with the blue of the sea in his eyes. 'I am hopeful that you will give us the pleasure of your voice, for it is true to say that sailors have a great fondness for the singing of the siren.'

Her smile faltered. 'I – I don't know if I'm in very good voice tonight, Captain.' But even as she spoke the curious feeling came over Della that she could sing again; it was as if in that Venetian garden of yesterday her own problems had seemed to diminish and seem hysterical rather than real. She loved to sing, she wanted to sing, and *la nonna* had urged her to be true to her own self when it came to singing.

Her left hand lifted of its own accord to her throat and the Captain's gaze followed the action and the gleaming of the ring on the third finger of her hand. 'Who,' he bent towards her, 'is the lucky man?'

'I am the lucky one.' She charmingly evaded a direct answer. 'I really think I might sing, if you have someone who could accompany me at the piano?'

There was a piano set at an angle against the silver-grey panelling of the lounge, which had blue leather banquettes, a blue-carpeted floor, and a glass bar decorated with exotic-bird motifs.

'Ladies and gentlemen,' the Captain raised his commanding voice, 'have we a pianist among us? Our lovely soprano guest has agreed to sing for us if someone can play her accompaniment?'

'Perhaps I can oblige?' drawled a voice from the doorway, and Della felt her heart skip a beat as Nick entered with Camilla at his side. 'I am no Rubinstein, but I am acquainted with the piano, and slightly acquainted with the lady.'

'No,' Della wanted to cry out, but already the Captain was escorting her in the direction of the piano. 'I – I should like a drink first,' she said, in a cornered voice. 'Drambuie, to smooth my throat.'

'Of course! I am so eager to hear you sing, Miss Neve.' The captain was charmingly apologetic even as he snapped his fingers at one of his young officers. 'Steve, a little Drambuie, and if there isn't any available at this bar, run and fetch some from the Tavern.'

'Yes, sir.' Steve went to the bar and sorted about among the bottles, and Della began to wish that she had stayed in her stateroom and hadn't appeared at the party as if she expected to be treated like a star. She strove not to look at Nick, but the compulsion was too strong to be fought and her eyes found him, at shoulder level, and she saw how hard and straight he held himself so that not a wrinkle showed in his white tuxedo. Her eyes lifted to his face, but his answering glance was perfunctory . . . he looked at her as if she were clad in a cotton shift instead of a highly flattering dress. Then he said something to Camilla and they began to cross the room in Della's direction.

How diamond-hard the woman was, thought Della. Capable of cutting a hole in a man's heart but of never filling the wound with warmth.

Nick inclined his head to the Captain and mentioned the fact that they had run into rough waters. 'I hope the weather will improve by morning,' he said. 'I plan to see Naples—'

'Or die, darling?' Camilla broke in with a husky laugh.

He answered her with a flickering, sardonic smile. 'Who knows?' he drawled. 'Fate can be a dramatic director and though we each like to believe that we direct our own course, it isn't truly so.'

'I shouldn't have taken you for a fatalist, *signore*.' The

Captain gave Nick a rather quizzical look. 'You appear to have taken life firmly by the horns, if I may say so? You seem a man who leaps in rather than waits – I understand, in fact, that you leapt into the kiddies' pool this morning and fished a youngster out of the water. I had it from the attendant who was feelng very guilty and upset and wanted a change of job. However, the very fact that this mishap occurred will keep her on her toes in future, but as I say, *signore,* I would list you as a man who holds a whiphand on life.'

'You make Nick sound rather cruel,' Camilla protested, pouting her lips at the Captain and accepting a cocktail from the tray which one of the stewards carried among the guests. 'It was my little girl whom he saved from drowning, and I'm desperately grateful to him.'

'How is Honey?' Della asked Camilla. 'I hope she is now over her fright?'

'Of course she is, Miss Neve. Children soon recover from their little ups and downs, as you will discover for yourself when you marry and have a child.'

'A while ago I was congratulating Miss Neve on her engagement,' said the Captain, gallantly handing to Della the slim glass of tawny-gold Drambuie which he had taken from the hand of Steve Ringdale.

'You're engaged?' Camilla focused her sharp glance on Della's left hand. 'Did that happen on board ship? I didn't notice before that you were wearing a ring. Who is the man? Anyone I know?'

'Well, he isn't on board this ship.' Della took a sip at her drink. 'This is very nice, Captain, and always very soothing to the voice. I am wondering if you have a special favourite when it comes to songs? I think it would be nice to let the choice be yours as you are in command of this delightful cruise we are all enjoying so much.'

'You're kind, Miss Neve!' For an instant the man in authority looked rather bowled over by the warm smile which Della directed at him; a smile that lit the blue lights in her eyes and curved her lips. 'I must confess that I'm not well up on classical music, but I am partial to songs from the musical shows. They seem more melodious to my sea-dog's ears.' He grinned engagingly. 'If you, a star of grand opera, wouldn't mind singing one of those?'

'It would be a pleasure, Captain.' Della spoke gaily, but she felt as if she were facing a greater challenge than her first role in grand opera, when Marsh's confidence in her ability as a singer had been as tangible as a hand reaching out to press her own hand. Right now she faced a roomful of ship's passengers, who held cocktail glasses and continued to discuss golf, fishing, and cocktail savouries, even as she made her way to the piano. The burly figure of the Captain walked at her side, and Nick strolled in their wake, tall and sardonic, and with that animal grace that made him stand out among other men. Everyone thought of him as hard, gay and self-ruled, and she had to pretend to believe the same.

When they reached the piano she swung to face Nick. 'There was an operetta showing in London about a year ago, *Amore, Giovanni*, which I thought was full of melody, and I am sure the Captain would enjoy one of the songs entitled *Me ne frego*. Do you know the music, *signore*? As you are an Italian I thought you might be acquainted with it?'

'Assuredly.' He sat down on the piano bench and ran his lean fingers along the keys, producing the gay and lilting music she spoke of. Then he glanced up at her, and his eyes were smiling wickedly. 'I notice that you choose the song in which the heroine tells Giovanni that she doesn't care a jot for him. I personally preferred the other popular song of the show.' And once again he played some of the melody. *Ti amo*. I love you!

Della turned instantly to the Captain and laid a

slightly flirtatious hand upon his braided cuff. 'I am sure you'll enjoy the song I have chosen to sing. The operetta concerned a man about town named Giovanni who becomes the guardian, though a gambling debt, of a young girl out of a convent. She attempts to reform him, and he attempts to inform her that love is the only thing that a girl should think about. In this particular song she tells him – for it's better if I sing it in the original Italian – that she knows all about his "ladies" and she doesn't care a jot if every woman in Rome is in love with him. It's a song I very much like, so let us hope, Captain, that my voice does it justice.'

'I am perfectly sure, Miss Neve, that you will sing like the angel you look.' And with old-fashioned gallantry the Captain kissed her hand, and then with a commanding frown he turned to his other guests and requested that they take seats and sit quietly while she sang to them. 'I know a cocktail party is for chit-chat,' he said, 'but this will make a nice change. I give you Miss Della Neve, accompanied at the piano by the Conte Nicholas di Fiori Franquila.'

A spate of clapping broke out and everyone sat down on the blue banquettes and the bar stools. Della flicked her gaze around the room and saw that Camilla was staring at her from her perch upon one of the stools, the slit skirt of her dark gold dress revealing a slim leg clad in skin-fine silk. Camilla had protested that Nick wasn't cruel, and Della wondered, for an instant, if he and the attractive divorcee were having an affair. Della didn't doubt for one moment that Nick would be a superb lover ... while the attraction held him; while the pleasure held at bay the pain.

She turned to Nick and her smile was her stage smile, gay and dazzling. She saw his eyes retreat with their secrets into the shadow of his lashes.

'Avanti, maestro,' she said. 'Shall we begin?'

His lean hands came down on the keys, as certain of the music as if he knew it by heart. And why not? she thought, as she waited for her cue. He had been taught as a boy to play, and she could imagine him, when his nights were lonely, seated at a piano in his New York apartment, playing all the Italian music he could recall . . . bringing the memories closer, and closer, until he slammed down the lid and went again in search of the carnival.

Came her cue and because she was thinking of Nick and not of herself she broke into song without any effort. Gone was the restriction, hers again was the ability to let her voice climb and climb with bell-like clarity into the high skies of sheer melody, which she so loved. Her heart bounded and her very soul seemed to sing in tune with her recovered voice.

Now there was not a murmur from her audience, not the faintest clink of a glass. The spell was cast and Della knew that she was singing as she had often longed to sing, as if only the emotion mattered and not the technique. She knew she was taking liberties with the melody, but Nick was following her, aiding her inventiveness, until suddenly it seemed quite natural for her to join him on the piano bench and to let him lead her into *Ti amo*, and other songs filled with the lyrical exhilaration of heart and enticement. It seemed that now she had started to sing again she couldn't stop, and a quick turn of her head brought her a glance from Nick and there was a smile, deep in his eyes, and for an instant her heart felt as if it might melt.

No! Impossible! Forbidden! Swinging her in panic to her audience, plumaged in bird-green, singing her heart out from the gilded cage that was invisibly locked about her.

As each song ceased, someone called out for another, and neither she nor Nick were at a loss. Old songs, new songs, and that spellbinding sense of rapport with the people to whom she sang.

Later that night, looking back on that impromptu concert, Della felt certain it had been the most satisfying *tour de force* of her career. And now, as always after a performance, she felt strung-up, restless, and disinclined to go to bed. If she were at home Rose, her maid, would have insisted that she drink Horlicks and take a sleeping pill, but she was far from home and the *Gothic Star* was still pitching, despite her stabilizers, and rain was beating down on the decks of the ship. There were also flickers of lightning over the sea, and Della felt as if the lightning was in her blood and acting like a magnet that suddenly made it impossible for her to remain cooped up in her stateroom.

She had not yet changed out of her dress, and snatching her cloak from the cupboard she threw it around her and pulled the hood, monk-like, over her hair and face.

The corridor leading from her stateroom was deserted and she had that feeling of having this great ship to herself as she walked silently along the blue corridor to the stairs. She was making for the glass-walled recreation-room on the sun-deck, which looked directly on to the water and would give her the feeling of being one with the storm without being half drowned by it. She took the self-service lift to the sun-deck and managed to avoid getting too wet as she ran the few yards to the recreation-room.

She felt excited, like a lonely cat on the prowl, and after throwing off her cloak she knelt in the window-seat, which was lined in scarlet leather, and gazed upon the heaving dark seas that were lit every few moments by the lightning. It had the gleam of steel until it touched the water, when it seemed to turn blue.

Della allowed her mind to slip back down the years, to that stormy night when she had sat like this in the bedroom of a strange house and the tears of grief and homesickness had run down her face just as the rain poured unrelentingly down the windowpanes.

He had told her that *they* were dead. He had such thick and glinting hair above his grey and glinting eyes. He frightened her a little, though she sensed that he was kind at heart. He said this big house was now her home, and this room of white rugs and cupboards and a bed covered by a blue satin quilt was hers to fill with books and playthings.

'Are you my foster-father?' she had asked him, and he had looked so odd and in a crisp voice he had corrected her.

'I am your guardian, child. From now on I take care of your health and your education, and you must think of me as a friend rather than a – a father. I am unmarried, you see. I am a bachelor.'

And so never again had she hinted that she would have felt much more at home with him had she been allowed to consider him a foster-parent rather than a guardian. To her youthful mind the word seemed to mean a guard, and the big house seemed full of things it seemed unwise of a child to touch. Lovely things all neat and quiet behind glass. Furniture so polished and so silky with damask that she kept her hands in her pockets in case she left finger-marks on the glossy surfaces. Carpets so deep and pale that she trod round the borders of them on the parquet, fearful of leaving traces of dirt from the covered terrace where she went, while it rained, to take some exercise.

And pianos! Two of them! A beautiful cream and gold one in the drawing-room, and a black grand in the music-room, where a famous Hebrew friend of his came to play such sad and haunting music. So sad that it made her run and hide in the flower-room. Only in the flower-room, with its sink, its clutter of flower vases and pots, and its smell of petals, did she feel really safe from the watchful house servants. There she could play about without the fear of breaking anything valuable.

It had been on a night like this, the darkness broken by flickers of lightning and rumblings of thunder up there in the sky where heaven was said to be, when she had wept in the window-seat of her Wedgwood room and Mr. Graham had entered so quietly to sit beside her in the seat. He had drawn her into his arms and pressed her wet and stormy face to the crisp whiteness of his dress-shirt. 'Tomorrow,' he had murmured, 'the rain will all be gone. We've been promised an end to this St. Swithin's bout of temperament, my dear. No more tears tomorrow, eh? Try to be happy, for it makes me happy to have you here in my rather lonely house.'

'I'll try, Mr. Graham.' She had hiccuped against his chest and felt terrified because her tear-wet face was marking his lovely shirt.

'You must call me Marsh.' He had stroked the tousled hair away from her brow and he had studied her face by the lightning. 'And from now on I shall call you Della.'

'Della?'

She came out of her reverie with a start, and the lightning seemed reflected in her wide eyes as she sat there against the flame-coloured leather in her velvet dress, gazing at Nick without any deep sense of surprise. It was as if her thoughts had prepared her for this moment, with the rain falling from the heavens and a man arriving in dress-jacket and shirt to say things that would have a deep effect on her life.

'What are you doing here at this hour?' He came with his silent tread across the recreation-room, and his eyes had an alert, hunting glow to them, as if it were natural for him to be about at night.

'I might as well ask you the same question, Nick.'

'I have been playing cards in the smoke-room. The session has just finished. And I felt like a solitary smoke before turning in.'

'Smoke, Nick,' she half-smiled. 'I shall try not to be too intrusive and will stay quiet as a mouse.'

'You are no mouse, *mia*.' The lightning flickered with the smile on his lips. 'More of a nightingale, I think. We drifted apart after our concert, but I wished to say that I have never heard you sing so well – the sea air has done wonders for you.'

'Thank you, Nick.' She leaned back in the window-seat and felt curiously adrift for a while from her anxieties. She watched as Nick lounged on the broad arm of a nearby chair and took from his jacket pocket his leather case of slim, dark cigars. There was a glimmer of white teeth as he bit the end, a sparkle of flame as he lit the cigar and jetted smoke from his nostrils.

'Nick,' she said, and her fingers played with her silk handkerchief, 'I had no idea that you had heard me sing before. You never mentioned the fact.'

'There are facts that I don't mention.' The words came lazily from his lips, with the aromatic smoke of his Havana. 'I resided in America and went now and again to San Francisco, so is it so very strange that I should go to the Opera House to listen to Italian opera? I heard you sing as Mimi and I admired your technique, but tonight, Dolly Neve, I heard you sing from the heart. It was an experience I am glad not to have missed, especially as I shall be leaving the *Gothic Star* tomorrow and we shall not be seeing each other again.'

Della had known from the moment of Nick's appearance that fate had somehow set the scene for a dramatic revelation from him, but she hadn't dreamed that it would be quite so stunning, so that her heart rocked and she only just managed to stop herself from crying out a protest. Never to see him again, devilish and infuriating as he was, charming and cruel as he could be!

There was a sudden sound of tearing silk and Della gazed in surprise at the two halves of her handkerchief.

'I am glad that you have not quite hated me,' Nick drawled. 'Actions they say speak more eloquently than words. I have spoken with the Captain and I shall not be continuing with the cruise – no, it is better, as *la nonna* said, for me to find my Italian roots once again. I tried to tear them out and the ache will always be there while I try to make my life elsewhere than in my own country. Tomorrow the ship docks at Naples and I shall be home once more, to stay. Home is where the heart is, and I am sure you will agree?'

As Nick ceased speaking his gaze dwelt on the ripped handkerchief, which she was gripping with her left hand, with its weight of jade and diamonds.

'You are right to return to Italy.' She forced her voice to be steady and reasonable. 'I shall miss you for the rest of the voyage, Nick. Our arguments have been stimulating, and I shall always have vivid memories of Venice.'

'If you enjoyed seeing Venice with me, then tomorrow let me show you something of southern Italy, and the thousand-band chorus of cicadas that make the warm hills seem alive and pulsing. I can hire a car and we can see Amalfi, Salerno and Sorrento. Each has something to offer, a hillside town, a Benedictine abbey, and the ruins of Pompeii. I know them as only an Italian can, so let me share them with you for a day? In a fast car I can have you back at the ship in time for the midnight sailing.'

Each word he spoke seemed like a tiny lifeline being thrown out to Della after that awful plunge she had taken, that awful feeling of a shock-wave sweeping over her. One more day, twelve hours stretched into a lifetime, before the *Gothic Star* left him behind in Italy and sailed off with her to other ports before the journey home to England. She had to clutch at what he offered, even though she knew that the lifeline must be severed in the end.

'Why not?' she said gaily. 'I've always wanted to see Naples. Tell me, Nick, why did the poet say "see Naples and die"?'

'Poets always exaggerate, and nothing ever really dies. A flower goes back into the ground, and places seen and people met adorn our minds, and our hearts, with their memorials.'

'Tonight, *signore*, you are very profound.'

'Tonight, *signorina*, I am very Italian.' He stubbed his cigar and reached for her cloak. 'Come, let me take you to your suite. You must have a good night's sleep and be in good form for tomorrow.'

Della rose to her feet and let him enfold her in the velvet cloak. He was very tall as he stood close to her, and she didn't dare to look at his face to see what it masked, or chose to reveal. They had never been so near to each other, nor as far apart.

'You should like Sorrento,' he said, as they walked out on to the sun-deck, which smelled of the rain which had died away. A cool, storm-washed breeze blew at them from the sea which still heaved a little, like a bosom after a storm of tears. When they reached the stairway, by passing the lift as if by mutual consent, they both glanced back a moment as if sharing the thought that never again would they walk together on the sun-deck, or duel with the words that flashed like sword-points around their secret selves.

They were descending the stairs when the ship heaved and Della would have stumbled if Nick had not caught hold of her. He drew her hard against him and the light of a wall-lamp flared on his face and Della saw a man who might have been a rather wonderful man if fate had not kicked the dreams out of his eyes and blinded him to tenderness for too long a time.

At the door of her stateroom they parted for the night. 'I shall see you *domani*.' He gave her a sudden formal and very Latin bow, drawing his heels together in the faintest click. '*Buona notte, signorina*, and sleep well.'

'Goodnight, *signore*.' She drew back into her stateroom, the hood of her cloak falling away from her ruffled fair hair, her eyes almost as green as the jade on her hand. 'And thank you for inviting me to share a little more of Italy with you.'

After he had gone and she had closed the door, she stood unmoving there and allowed the realization to sweep over her that this time tomorrow night he would be a memory; a shipboard acquaintance come and gone. And that was life ... life that '*drew iron tears down Pluto's cheek, And made Hell grant what love did seek*'.

CHAPTER EIGHT

DELLA'S training in opera, with its disciplines and its insistence on control of body and mind, paid off for her the morning the *Gothic Star* anchored in the Bay of Naples.

She had rolls and coffee in her stateroom, showered and dressed with care, and then went on deck to join the passengers who were going ashore on the tender. The storm and wind of last night had happily passed on their way and the sea and skies were bright and beckoning.

Della saw Nick the moment she stepped on to the departure deck. She watched him a moment as he stood at the rail edge and gazed at the white terraces of Naples and the cone of Vesuvius rising above the town in the background. Della ached with an infinite deep pain, for Nick and for herself, then he turned around as if he felt her eyes upon him, and instantly she wooed a smile to her lips.

He smiled as his gaze passed over her, taking in the pale-coloured dress she wore, with a deep hem of coloured silks woven into a striking pattern. A deep-brimmed hat shaded the blue-green sorcery of her eyes, and her only adornment was a neckchain holding a coral charm. Her heartbeats quickened as Nick's eyes registered the fact that she had left off her engagement ring, his eyelids narrowing until his lashes completely concealed his expression.

He came towards her and she felt that emanation of danger, and desire. 'You look more beautiful than I have seen you look before,' he said. 'As if you had just stepped out of the frame of a modern-day Gainsborough. Italy, *signorina,* will fall in love with you.'

'Grazie, signore.' Her heart had instantly warned her that it had been a mistake to remove her ring, for now she had underlined the significance of this, their last day together. It was as if she told him without words that today they forget everyone and live only for themselves.

Tilting her chin, playing the *diva*, she gave a laugh. 'You look very distinguished yourself, Nick.' She flicked her eyes over his wine-coloured suit and pale-grey shirt with a silky sheen to it. His black hair was smooth as a hawk's wing, with that faint sheen of silver over the temples. 'Very much the lordly gentleman of Italy.'

At once his lashes lifted and she caught the full force of his gaze, exciting and dangerous, so that she almost turned on her heel and fled from him. He seemed to sense that this might happen and he reached out for her hand, gripping it, letting her know that he meant to have this day with her.

'Andiamo,' he murmured. 'You made a promise and must keep it.'

'Very well, Nick.' She smiled and tried not to feel his touch in her very bones. 'Shall we join the others? They're about to go aboard the tender.'

It was in the queue of disembarking passengers that they came face to face with Camilla, who had Honey with her, and a steward carrying a couple of suitcases. Honey was full of chatter about her grandfather, whom she and her mother were meeting on the dock. Nick swung the child to his shoulder and he studied her young face rather earnestly. 'You are happy to be going with your grandfather to live?' he asked her. 'You will become almost an Italian young lady, eh?'

'Grandpapa has a vineyard, Nick,' she told him eagerly. 'It is, you will never guess, near the big mountain that is full of lava.'

'Vesuvius?' he smiled. 'Yes, the grapes grow big and fat

up there, for the soil feeds from the long-dead lava. The *ginestra* hills are up there, all golden in the summer time. It is good to live in Italy, little one.'

Camilla stared at Nick, as if seeing what Della had seen, that he was entirely Italian today, with not a hint of that suave cosmopolitan in his manner and his smile. 'Nostalgia for Italy does have you in its grip,' Camilla said to him, and there was a tightness about her lips as her glance flickered to Della and then back again to Nick. 'I could have spent the day with you, but my father-in-law will expect me to spend a few hours at the villa, while Honey settles in.'

'That is only natural, on both counts,' he said, rather crisply. Then he looked again at Honey and brushed a kiss across her cheek. 'We will say *arrivederci* for now, *cara*, but I will come and see you one day at the vineyard of your grandpapa. How will you like that?'

'Oh, Nick!' The child tightened her arms about his neck. 'Will you really?'

'Yes indeed. It will be fun, eh?'

'Nick, don't make that sort of promise,' Camilla broke in. 'Honey will expect you to keep it.'

'And I intend to keep it.' His eyes met Camilla's. 'I am staying on in Italy and leaving the ship today. My luggage is being taken to the Francesco Hotel in Naples, where I shall stay overnight, travelling on to Tuscany in the morning. The time has come for me to go home – do you know those lines of Browning's? "*Open my heart and you will see, Graved inside of it, Italy*".'

'And I wonder how long you'll last, Nick?' Camilla gave him a long, challenging look. 'You aren't going to find very much fun or diversion in the wilds of Tuscany, for I shouldn't imagine there are many smart restaurants or clubs in that vicinity, least of all the sort of women for whom you have acquired a taste. Don't tell me you are planning to live like a monk, Nick? Or have you a local *amata* who has devotedly waited for you all this time? I have heard that Italians usually end up marrying a girl chosen for them!'

Della held her breath as Camilla unwittingly struck at Nick's secret, and deepest wound. But all he said, perhaps because he held Honey and would not be angry in front of her, was that they should go aboard the tender. It was a relief for Della when they docked and Nick said good-bye to Honey, who then rushed at Della for a hug and a kiss. 'Will you come with Nick?' the child asked, as all around them on the dock people milled and talked in a mixture of languages. 'When he comes to see me?'

And the answer which Della had to give was still between Nick and herself when they sat in the supercharged coupé which he hired for this last day they would ever share.

They swiftly left behind them the animated, colourful and confusing centres of Naples, heading for the autostrada that led to Salerno. *'O dolce Napoli, O suol beato,'* Nick murmured. 'Naples is the heaven and the hell in the soul of the Italian.' They sped along an esplanade flanked by gardens and old *palazzi*, one of which Nick pointed out as the house where Admiral Nelson had first fallen in love with Lady Hamilton.

'For many Italy has been the land of love. But for others,' Nick shrugged and swung the car past the *piazzetta* of a church where he said Shelley had had christened a small girl which might have been his, for he had given her his own name. They then passed through the district of La Torretto, where long ago had stood a look-out tower for the warning of the residents that Barbary pirate ships had been sighted.

A few more miles and they were in the countryside and the warm air smelled of stone walls in the sun, fresh bread from the farmstead ovens, and the tang of herbs on the hillsides. They travelled past olive groves and terraced vines, and old ruins like ghosts in the sun.

'Shall we bypass Pompeii and go on to Ravello?' Nick asked suddenly. 'I am not in the mood for what is past and ruined, are you?'

She felt the double meaning in his words, though he couldn't know that she had been let into the secret of his own past. 'I like the sound of Ravello,' she said at once. 'I believe Caruso came from there, didn't he?'

'It could be so. Della, sing for me now! Anything, a favourite of yours, for it is said that if you sing in Italy you will always sing, and I like to think that you will remember today when you sing again in England.'

'Nick – I couldn't.' Her throat was hurting her, for when she sang again in England this sad, lovely, immortal day would be over, and like the asphodels on the hills it would be just a memory. The English sky would never be so blue, nor the air smell of wine and honey. There would be no oleanders gone wild, nor hills haunted by lonely olive trees. There would be no more the brush of a wine-coloured sleeve and the play of dark eyes over her face.

'Take off your hat,' Nick ordered, 'take a deep breath of air and sing just for me. Come, I don't make you shy, do I?'

'Heavens, no.' She obediently unpinned her hat and let loose her hair, which the sun quickly found and set shining. 'Why should I be shy of one man when I have sung for thousands?'

'Why indeed?' he drawled. 'Now you have found your voice again you should exercise it. Sing!'

'You sound as bullying as my old music master,' she retorted.

'Was he an Italian?'

'What else!' She gave a slightly tormented laugh. 'What would you have me sing, tyrant? It seems I am at your mercy, miles from anywhere, in the depths of your Sabine countryside.'

'You know the story of the Sabines?'

'Yes, I am old enough for that.'

'And old enough to wed a man. Why did you leave off your ring?'

'I can soon replace it. I have it in my purse.'

'No, leave it where it is. I understand why you felt you could not wear today the love token of another man. It is a token of love, eh?'

'Yes.' A note of restraint came into her voice. 'No man could be as good to me as Marsh has been and not – love me.'

'I have heard that he's a tough character when it comes to business. Does he bully you?'

'No!'

'Your denial is very emphatic, Dolly.'

'My name is Della. Marsh had it changed legally a long time ago.'

'I can't help but wonder why. Dolly is such a girlish and kissable name.'

'Please, Nick!'

'Please, *nina*?' He cast her a mocking sideglance. 'What would you like from me?'

'An end to this inquisition. I care for Marsh – he has been the greatest influence on my life – and he needs me.'

'And what do you need, Della?'

'Happiness, like most people.'

'What if I might also have a need for – someone?'

'There are lots of women to satisfy your needs, Nick. They have nothing to do with the heart.'

'What would you know of my heart? I keep it firmly locked against lovely innocents like you.'

'You also keep it locked against the Camillas in your life. You told me yourself, Nick, that love for you is a matter of a day and a night. No more than a session at the gaming table, or a meal at the Ritz. You partake of love as if it were a buffet of caviare and champagne, and then you stroll on to a race meeting, or an evening at the opera. I don't blame you, Nick! But will you really settle down in Tuscany after so long at the fair?'

'I shall try, and if I fail the fair is always there to welcome me back.'

'Oh, Nick—'

'You sound so pained, *nina*, as if you feel sorry for me.' His tone of voice hardened. 'Don't waste your pity on a man who has made his own bed of nails.'

'But you didn't make it—' She broke off, realizing that she had almost said too much. 'I mean, there is usually a reason why someone goes astray, and I expect you have your reason.'

'Oh, it's always "because",' he drawled. 'Now there is a cue for a song, if I ever heard one! Della, do you know it?'

'Yes—' The road they were driving along was winding upwards above a breathtaking valley filled with orchards and the silvery foliage of olive trees, and she knew they were bordering Sorrento, the lotus-land of Italy. It was all so beautiful, and all to be seen only this one time with Nick, that Della felt moved to tell him that she knew about Donaleza, his arranged marriage, and the death of his daughter. She wanted truth between them, not a valley of rocks where they stumbled around the truth, avoiding it and bruising each other in the process. She almost spoke, but from under her lashes she saw the adamantine set of his chin, clefted with shadow. She saw his lips set firmly, and felt her own fear of the anger she might arouse in him. All he wanted was a day snatched out of time . . . the two of them happy for a while, with no yesterday, and no tomorrow.

So as they drove above the valley filled with the perfume of oranges Della sang for him a love song that could never come true.

She sang to the music of the birds and the speeding wheels of the car, and as the last notes died away and they slowed on a bend of the road, Nick reached for her hand and thanked her with a kiss on each finger.

The action was so courtly, so much nicer than words, that Della felt a whimsical longing to believe that never before had Nick kissed a woman in quite that way.

'You needed to come to Italy to find your true voice,' he said.

She smiled in answer to him, and knew that in exchange for her voice she had lost much of her heart.

With Sorrento behind them, the landscape became wilder and lost the grace and garden beauty of the place whose very walls seemed to smoke with scent in the sun. Now they drove along a wide stretch of coast, rising above a sea that was a blazing mass of water-flames, circling into a rugged *corniche* that seemed as if it had dug itself out of the great cliffs, providing spectacular views and making the heart race. This went on for miles, straight through the heart of sleepy villages, almost Saracen, with whitewashed houses framed in thick walls and flat roofs. A coastline raped in the old days by Barbary corsairs, so that it wasn't truly surprising that the eastern look should linger.

The air blew like the tang of a strong and intoxicating wine, and Della delighted in the feel of it in her face and her hair, which had now blown out of its neat styling and was free and bright about her flushed face.

She felt a sense of rapture and could not forbid it, today of all days, to go away. She opened her eyes and her heart to it, and journeyed as if through space with Nick. It seemed so, for they were high above the sea and travelling swiftly towards Amalfi. 'Hungry?' Nick flung at her, through the rushing of the wind. 'We could lunch at Amalfi and save Ravello for the afternoon.'

'I am in your hands,' she laughed, brushing a wing of

hair from her eyes, which were the colour of the sea and filled with the same sunlit sparkle. 'This is your Italy, Nick, so you know best what we should do, and how much time we have to spare.'

'Let us pretend that we have a thousand years,' he quipped. 'Lunch, then, at the first interesting place we come upon.'

This turned out to be a *ristorante* of flower-hung stone, where they chose a table in the garden, set near an archway looking on to the pink-washed houses and lemon gardens of Amalfi. They ate giant prawns roasted with lemon, dark crisp bread with butter, and a tangy white wine. Bees hummed among the flowers that crusted the walls of the garden, and Della ate her food, opposite Nick who had discarded his jacket and tie, and who sat there, white teeth biting dark bread, with the same air of Latin virility as the fishermen and lemon-workers who came here to eat fish and strong cheese with onion, all washed down with a strong wine of the province. Was this just a sun-dream, she wondered, and would she wake in a while to find herself alone? Suddenly she reached out with her wine glass and let it clink against Nick's, and the sound was real, his swift, quizzical smile was real, and so was a growl of laughter from a nearby table.

'*Bene*,' said Nick. 'The wine is *dolce, si*?'

'*Si.*' She smiled and drank and let it go to her head. She didn't want to care what Marsh would think if he could see her right now, sitting here among fishermen, her hair all tousled about her face, eating prawns and drinking wine with a man who was an admitted rake. She played with a flame, and saw it smouldering in Nick's eyes as they played over her bare neck and arms.

Suddenly he was leaning forward and looking keenly at her unguarded face. 'How nice to be Apollo and free to kiss you wherever you are free to be kissed.'

'Apollo?' She dipped a prawn in lemon sauce and tried

to look more innocent than she felt. 'It must be the wine, because I don't get you.'

'God of the sun. See how he plays with your hair and strokes your neck. No mortal man is allowed to be so daring, for he would have his face slapped, eh?' Nick's teeth gleamed against the Italian darkness of his face. 'Today you are like Proserpina, both innocent and nervously aware of everything around you. You admire the rose yet you know its roots to be twisted. You see the hawk-moth swoop on the ladybird. You are alive to all this exquisite cruelty and it hurts, eh?'

'Yes,' she admitted. 'But wasn't Proserpina swooped on by Aidoneus, who rode up out of the flowers in his dark chariot?'

'Lord of the dark,' Nick drawled, his eyes fixed upon Della's. 'The most ruthless of all the gods, eh? Only the virginal Proserpina could brighten his dark world for a while. Yes, just for a while.' Then, as if his dark memories flared into active pain, he snapped his fingers for the waiter and their second course was hurried to them.

Half an hour later they were off in the car again, Nick's jacket flung to the back seat with Della's hat and bag. The sun was riding high and only the rush of the wind saved them from being scorched as they sped along the mountain road to Ravello.

Della sat silent, enjoying the drive until they reached the Valle delle Dragone, with its look of a world lost in hanging gardens and old sprawling villas, with columns green with foliage. Della caught her breath and felt a wild stirring of her emotions, and as if in answer to her unspoken plea Nick brought the car to a halt and it clung there against the mountainside, and they were as if tucked beneath a wing of the cliffs.

'And there lies beauty, which the modern world has not yet ravished.' Nick spoke very quietly, one hand on the wheel, and the other arm stretched along the seat behind

Della's shoulders. 'It was worth the long drive, eh?'

'Yes,' she murmured, and she was very still in her seat, not making a movement that might break the spell. Also she was aware that any slight movement might bring her into physical contact with Nick and such a contact, while she was made so vulnerable by the beauty of the valley, might be inflammable. All day, right up to this moment, there had been this awareness between them, and because it was a thing of the senses it had to be fought even if it could not be ignored.

'There is a fine old *palazzo* at the other side of the valley which you might care to see.'

'That would be nice.' Della could feel him looking at her, and she didn't dare to return his look. His eyebrow would be quirked, his mouth would wear that slightly mocking and indulgent curve, and the grey silk of his shirt would be opened against the brown strength of his throat. Della would see all this and there would go winging through her that treacherous urge to be gathered close against his lean and exciting body.

'Yes, do let us go and see the *palazzo*.' She found the handle of the car door and pressed it downwards, and quickly stepped out on to the grass. She told herself wildly that what she felt for Nick was impurely physical ... something she was experiencing for the first time in her guarded life, and she just had to get through this day without giving in to it. It would be a draught of wild wine, a forbidden rapture, followed by the awful regret that she had broken faith with Marsh ... dear, strong, generous Marsh, who had waited so patiently to become the lover of his Galatea.

She and Nick scrambled their way down the hillside, clinging to clumps of herb and rock in their descent to the gardens and terraces of the old palace, which had a mediEval courtyard, patterned by tiles in which the device of the family had been stamped. They climbed the courtyard steps to the terrace that overlooked the surrounding countryside, and it was then that Nick told her about his home in Tuscany, which he said was a rambling house upon a hilltop, which equally magnificent views over the Tuscan fields and valleys.

'When dusk falls and the moonflowers open on their vines, it is very quiet up there, with only the cicadas purring in the trees. I have a *terrazzo* much like this one, and it is peaceful to sit there, with a humidor of cigars at hand.' Nick pressed his hands down over the stone coping of this terrace on which he stood with Della, and she saw the knuckles of his hands slowly whiten under the brown skin. In the quietness of those Tuscan evenings he would be haunted by memories, and he knew it. There would be no gay carnival to drown the tormenting whispers and the scream of the drowning.

'Yes, with the fall of dusk everything is so fragrantly cool after the heat of the day. Cool like the sound of a fountain, like the petals of the moonflowers, and the pale skin of a strange woman. The moths fly about like ghosts ...' He broke off with a harsh sigh and abruptly his left hand was gripping Della's, and she didn't fight him, for she knew he had need of a spar as the memories swept over him. After several moments he looked at her hand and slowly loosened his grip as he saw the pressure marks on her skin. 'What a fragile thing is a woman's hand, and yet in some ways how strong. It rocks the cradle, soothes the brow, and sometimes it kills. These two fingers,' he played with the fourth and fifth fingers of her hand, 'the marriage and death symbols. And within the palm the warmth and the slap. And here at the wrist the pulse and the veins leading to the heart. A woman holds happiness and hope in her hand, and sometimes eternal damnation.'

'Don't, Nick! Oh, please, don't go on tormenting yourself!' The words broke from Della and wouldn't be held back. 'I can't bear to see you like this—'

'Like what?' Suddenly his face was savage, as if he might strike her for the pity in her voice. 'What the hell are you talking about? What is tormenting me? That you belong to some other man?'

'No!' She cried out as if he slapped her. 'I'm no part of what hurts you so badly. As if I would think so!'

'Then what are you thinking?' His hands leapt to grip and hold her by the shoulders, and his fingers felt as if they were burning her skin. 'We've talked in riddles long enough, you and I. Are you my torment, and are you preparing to put me out of my agony?'

'Don't!' She flinched in the face of the devil she had let loose in him. 'I – I know about your little girl. Your grandmother told me how you – lost her.'

'Lost her?' he gritted. 'To lose something implies that it can be found again, but I can never find Trini again. She lived so short a time, and she died forever. But how would you understand what it feels like to have a part of yourself torn out? You have been cocooned for too long a time in the silk nest made for you by a rich collector of beautiful, perfect things. Your day always started with a rose on a silvery tray, and ended with a chaste kiss on the cheek. What would you know of love?'

'What would you know of it?' she flung back at him. 'You married to suit your father, as I shall marry a man who has been good to me. Love has more than one face – sometimes it has a kind face.'

'There is another kind,' he taunted her. 'And neither of us has found that. The kind that lasts till the sun grows cold, and the stars are old, and the leaves of the judgment book unfold. Don't tell me the jade ring implies such a love for you.'

'It implies trust, affection, mutual respect. Those are good qualities, and far more lasting than a mere hunger of the senses—'

'Is it a hunger of the senses which I arouse in you?' The look which he swept over her was so insolent that it was unbearable, and she wrenched aside from him so suddenly that his fingers tore the fine silk of her dress and his fingernails ripped her pale, fine skin. She gave a cry of sheer pain, and the next moment she was stumbling down the terrace steps to the courtyard and running wildly to the half-open gate. All she wanted was to get away from the devil in Nick, but there was no place to go but the car, and if she could reach it before him, she would drive it herself, back along that mountain road with the sea as her guide.

But Nick was long-legged, agile and angry, and he caught up with her as she was scrambling her way up the hillside to where the coupé stood with the red glow of the sunset on its bodywork. 'Della!' Nick gripped her left ankle with his hand and made her sprawl among the long-headed herbs and the thyme, captive as any Sabine, with tears spilling down her face. He knelt beside her, his arms across her body. 'Don't be a child,' he said roughly. 'Don't cry, for yourself, or for me.'

'Y-you don't care who you hurt,' she said, the tears running into her hair, and down the slope of her cheekbone. 'You chase off everyone who would be y-your friend. You slap away the hand that would like to offer you a little sympathy – only a little, Nick, because I know that nothing anyone can do can turn back the pages of the judgment book. I lost my father and my mother, and I care for Marsh because he tried so hard to make up for their loss. I let him try, but you have never allowed anyone to do that for you, Nick.'

'Perhaps I have reserved that privilege for you.' He brought his face down close to Della's and she saw the little flames of purgatory in his eyes. 'Come, Della, burn with the memories, the fallen leaves of time. Be the little martyr with me, as you plan to be so with Marsh

Graham. *Cielo*, a pair of sacrifices will surely put you in favour with the angels.'

'Damned devil!' she cried. 'You've lived in hell so long that you're no longer completely human. I know what you can do to me, and I know the limits of my strength—'

'It would be Sabine history repeating itself, eh? And you are not going to beg and plead your way out of my arms?'

She gazed up scornfully at him, even while her heart thudded its panic beneath the pressure of his arm. His face this close to her was as wickedly fascinating as she first remembered it, but what had been added was a look so ruthless that it might have been the face of a devil . . . uncaring of anything but making a woman pay the price of what had led him into hell. Her head seemed to swim and she seemed to lose awareness of everything but the sudden warm crush of the mocking lips on hers, the feel of the hard body holding her to the crushed herbs, the molten flow of the sunset against her closed eyelids. If it was hell, it was also heaven, the wild, warm, male lips passing all over her face and down against her throat, his smothered words reaching her senses if not her ears. The incense of the herbs rose all about them, and her will to resist was like the sun going down, flushed and tormented, her golden head thrown back in an attempt to elude the lips that seemed to know exactly where she was most vulnerable and nervous.

He would not have let her go, she knew that . . . it was something more primitive than even he that tore them apart for just a moment . . . a rushing sound of rocks suddenly torn loose from the ground and set tumbling on their heavy, jagged course down the hillside.

The earth rocked, everything moved, and with the oath of the Italian who has felt this kind of commotion before in his life, Nick rolled over and over, with Della clasped to him, out of the path of the rocks which the earth tremor had disturbed.

Now to be locked in Nick's arms was a different sort of experience, shielded with him by a hummock in the ground as the earth beneath them seemed to billow and heave for moments on end. 'The *terremoto*,' he breathed in her ear. 'This is how it comes, like the fist of Jupiter crashing down and shaking us all by the scruff of the neck.'

'You – you deserve it,' she choked, and all at once her face was pressed to his shoulder and she was laughing ... laughing with her release from the emotions which had been unbearably aroused, torn naked from the cool recesses of the composed person she had been taught to be.

'You have more courage for the earthquake than you have for me, eh?' His fingers stroked upwards through her hair, against the roots, making them tingle as if she were a cat. 'Your fiancé might have made a lady of you, but he has forgotten to take into account that at heart you are a girl of the people. Come, the tremor is passing, and so is time. If I am to get you back to the ship by midnight, then we must drive very fast.'

He helped her to her feet and as she brushed the grasses from her dress, everything was strangely still again. As they walked to the car, she raised her face to the sky that was a rather ominous dark red. 'I must thank you, Lord Jupiter,' she said.

Nick smiled sardonically as he opened the car door. 'Would it have been so terrible?' he drawled. 'In this permissive age?'

'I am not a permissive person,' she said, taking her seat. 'Will the tremors return, Nick?'

'Which ones?' he asked, and she heard him laugh in his throat as he took his own seat and pressed the switch that raised the roof of the coupé and folded it down. Now they were enclosed together in the intimacy of the car, and outside the Italian night was falling, mantling the hills which had been so rudely disturbed only a few minutes ago. The car engine leapt into life and warmth began to come from the heater.

'Are you going to be warm enough?' Nick asked her. 'We have a long drive ahead of us and when the sun dies, the heat of the day dies with it.'

'I shall be all right—' She was confused by his concern, for it followed too closely upon his wilful lovemaking.

'Reach for my jacket,' he ordered, 'and put it around you.'

'You'll want it—'

'Do as you are told, *nina*.'

'Very well.' She leant over to the back seat and took hold of his jacket, which was smooth to the touch, the wine-coloured material lined with grey silk which made her shiver slightly as it brushed her arms, and the bared part of her shoulder where her dress had been torn by Nick.

'Is that better?' he asked, making a smooth turn on the road, which was luckily free of rocks, most of which had tumbled down the hillside below the road.

'Yes, thank you.' A note of constraint had come into her voice . . . in his arms she had been at the mercy of his angry passion, but right now, wrapped in a garment of his, she was at the mercy of her own compassion. The material enclosing her was redolent of his cigar smoke, and the image of the way he had looked, standing at the ship's rail, a look about him of a man lost in a very personal loneliness. Her fingers clenched the jacket and she pulled the collar up about her throat.

They had pased through the shuttered villages of Sorrento, and were descending the road at a good pace, the light of their headlamps fanning out ahead of them to show the way, when all at once there loomed in their path what looked like half a mountain ripped off and flung down in front of them. Nick flung on the brakes and they came to a halt a second or two before they would have hit the landslide.

'Chè triste, chè disastro!' Nick exclaimed. 'Will you look at that! The car would have to be a tractor to climb over that hill!'

Disaster indeed! Della peered forward and took in the blockage which loomed dark in the light of their lamps. The whole mess of rock and clumps of broken earth sprawled to the very edge of the road, spilling over and sealing off their progress so effectively that all they could do was turn to each other and look rather lost.

'We should have to return to Amalfi and take the other road,' he said, 'and even then I could not get you back in time for the midnight sailing.'

'You mean we're stranded, in the middle of nowhere?'

'You can see it. The tremors must have struck here with more force and brought down several tons of rubble. I can attempt to back the car until it is comparatively safe to turn around, but it will be risky on such a narrow road.'

'And what is the alternative, *signore*?' Somehow she had to be formal, for the situation had taken on risky aspects – in more ways than one. 'Do we stay here all night in the car?'

He sat thoughtful a moment, the engine quiet now, and only the tapping of his fingers on the wheel to break the silence. Then abruptly he spoke. 'With the engine shut off there is no warmth from the heater, and if I keep the engine running we will be out of gas by the morning. No! I think our best plan would be to find habitation and beg a night's lodging. I am sure we passed a house a mile or two back, and it shouldn't take us long to find it again. Well, *signorina*, what do you say?'

'It seems an excellent idea to me—'. But her face was pensive in the slanting light of the dashboard. 'It will be a nuisance missing the boat. The next port of call is one of the Greek islands, so I should have to fly there to join the ship. Oh dear!'

'Are you thinking of the fiancé and what he will say?' drawled Nick. 'You are going to be foolish enough, or honest enough to tell him, eh?'

'I – I've always told Marsh everything. He admires honesty, and we are only guilty of being caught in the middle of an earthquake. If I don't tell him, he may hear the story from someone else, and you know how people embellish a bit of—' She broke off, biting her lip.

'Scandal?' The word came with the smoothness of silk or steel. 'It would inevitably be scandalous for a girl to be alone for the night with Nick Franquila. Well, my advice to you, *nina*, is to keep this episode to yourself. I would be the last man on earth to deny my own reputation, and I should hate to break up a true romance.'

'Don't be sarcastic,' she flashed. 'Because you have no principles doesn't mean that the principles of other men are – are narrow. Anyway, I think we should go looking for that house before we end up having an argument that will make things seem even more uncomfortable than they are.'

'Sweet child, I did not cause the earth tremor. I may very well be in league with Satan, but I have never been to Olympus and met Jupiter. Come, shall we brave *la notte bruna* together? It may worry you to remain alone in the car while I go searching for shelter.'

They left the car standing all alone in the shadow of the landslide, and still wearing Nick's jacket around her shoulders – he refused the return of it almost brusquely – she walked with him through the darkness that became less so as their eyes accustomed themselves to it. The starlight was obscured by the clouds that were riding the sky, and now and again below the road edge a night bird cried, as if disturbed by the sound of their footfalls.

'The night speaks of different things to people,' said Nick, after they had walked in silence for a while. 'What does it say to you, *nina*? Does it unnerve you, or excite you? Does it whisper of beauty or menace?'

'Right now of hunger, I'm afraid.' She gave a slight laugh, for she didn't wish to be drawn into an emotive discussion with him, not right now, when she was so alone with him and there was no chance of getting back to the *Gothic Star*. His height, for instance, always made her feel rather defenceless, but as they walked along he seemed to tower beside her in her low-heeled shoes. The wind fluttered the sleeves of his shirt, and there was a dark, piratical grace to him, a careless salute to fate that this should happen to them. He had the kind of reputation that could not be damaged, but she – Della shivered and drew his jacket closer about her.

'Look!' He suddenly gestured at a pair of iron gates set back from the road and revealed by a queer flickering light.

'Will-o'-the-wisp,' she gasped. 'But I thought – don't they haunt wasteland and empty places?'

'We must hope that the house is inhabited,' he said, pushing at the gates so they groaned. 'This seems to be the only house around and we can't keep walking. Chin up, *nina*. You might soon be eating hot *pizza* for your supper. Think of it!'

'Don't, Nick,' she begged, for it now seemed hours since they had eaten and the thought of hot, meaty *pizza* was almost more than she could bear.

'Hold my hand.' He held out his hand and she had to take it. 'This courtyard seems very much overgrown and I don't want you to trip and fall.'

His fingers gripped hers as they made their way across the wide quadrangle of the court, among the tangles of foliage which had spread from the parent shrubs and trees growing against the walls that seemed to be very high. Nick seemed to have an inner eye for the geography of these old courts, but Della had the feeling they had stepped into some benighted villa where only ghosts were in residence.

She was proved correct, for when they reached the front door and found the iron bell-pull, the hollow ringing sound which it made in the interior of the place brought no one to their assistance. The neglected courtyard was an obvious sign of the owner's absence, and Della could have wept with disappointment. She had so hoped that they would find warm sanctuary for the night, but instead they knocked on the door of an empty house and disturbed only an owl keeping his vigil in the great gable above the door.

'The place is unoccupied,' said Nick, 'but it will provide a roof for the night if I can find a window to open.'

'Nick, I—' Della looked about her and saw shadows everywhere and the dark shapes of straggling shrubs. 'I don't much fancy staying here.'

'We have not much alternative, *nina*.' He spoke in a firm voice, letting her know that he would brook no feminine scruples. 'We can't keep walking about in the dark, and I have to confess that I am feeling the cold, as most Latins do when the sun goes down.'

'Oh, Nick, you make me feel guilty – I have your coat—'

'You are welcome to my coat, but now we have found something resembling a household we are going to make the most of it. Now stay here, right here, while I take a look at the lower windows and attempt a way in. As the place is deserted we shall not be accused of trespass. You will do as I say?'

'Let me come with you?' she pleaded. 'It's so dark—'

'The darkness can't hurt you, so don't become emotional at a time like this. You actually laughed during the *terremoto*. Did that hold less terror for you than staying here in this deep porch while I add to my black arts by becoming a housebreaker.' Suddenly his fingers were gripping her chin and she saw the dark shine of his eyes as he gazed down at the pale shape of her face. 'What an irrational creature you are, to shiver at a shadow and endure real danger with a sense of humour! I shall leave you alone for no more than a few minutes, but I am flattered that for once you don't wish to be left alone by me.'

'You do indeed flatter yourself.' She pulled away from him with a jerk of her head, and she heard him laugh low in his throat. Then he had left her all alone and she could hear him rustling in the shrubs like a great animal, seeking the windows of the villa in the hope of finding a loose catch, or one that would yield to the blade of his pocket-knife. She drew back into the porch as his footfalls faded away around the great bulk of the building, and she could hear the leaves of the trees whispering around her, and the cold touch of the wind against her silk-clad legs.

What a day this one had been! And now it was to be followed by a night alone with Nick, that good-bye on the dock of Naples held at bay by circumstances beyond their control. She peered at the little jewelled dial of her wrist-watch and caught her breath. It was almost eleven o'clock and in one hour's time the ship would set sail without her, and Joe Hartley would report to the Captain that she had not come aboard. Joe would be the one to do that because he would be concerned for her welfare. Questions would be asked of the other passengers who had gone ashore for the day, and Camilla would be bound to say that she had seen Della with Nick Franquila.

Oh lord! Della closed her eyes against the image of the scandalized glances when it was disclosed that she had spent the day in the company of the notorious Conte, and by her non-appearance proved that she was probably spending the night with him as well. Such a snack of gossip would be handed around on a plate, and by morning she would no longer be referred to as the cool Miss Neve. It would be assumed that Nick Franquila had melted her reserve and kept her with him in Naples.

Oh, it wasn't the gossip she so much minded – for she knew the truth of the situation – it was that a twisted verion of the truth should get to the ears of Marsh. She knew how much trust he placed in her, and this Italian adventure would seem like a betrayal of that trust.

Lost in her thoughts she gave a startled cry as bolts were drawn on the inside of the door where she stood. She drew away as it was opened, and standing there in the aperture, a lamp in his hand, was the tall figure of Nick. The wick of the lamp flickered and threw his shadow on to panelled hall walls, while Della was revealed in the doorway, cloaked in the grey jacket, the pupils of her eyes enlarged like a cat's as she blinked at Nick.

'I got in by a kitchen window,' he said, 'and I found this lamp hanging on the wall and still quite full of oil. Come along in, Della. Tonight we have the place to ourselves, though I should imagine someone comes in during the daytime to dust the cobwebs and make coffee. The kitchen cupboard is not entirely bare, and there is a basket of firewood so the stove can be lit. The owners may be absent abroad, or the villa may be for sale. In either case we are fortunate to have the use of the place for the night. Come, don't stand there. Come in out of the cold.'

She obeyed him and entered the hall, which was of gothic proportions rising to a great dome of a ceiling frescoed with coats of arms and winged figures. Revealed in only a shadowy way by the lamplight they seemed oddly menacing up there, as if poised to fly down on the two intruders.

'It's quite an imposing sanctuary,' drawled Nick. 'Look at the marble floor and the woodwork, and those marquetry cabinets set against the walls. They are empty now, but would probably have held the family treasures. Relax, *nina.* It is better than a cowshed!'

'I know.' She forced a laugh. 'But I'm not used to – to this sort of thing.'

'I don't exactly make a habit of it,' he said dryly, 'and I am sure the Italian owners will not begrudge us the use of their fireplace and their kitchen. Hospitality is a Latin virtue, and we do have a few of those. I suggest—'

And there he broke off, for as he spoke he had been playing the light of the lamp around the hall and it had suddenly fallen upon a wide, padded settle that stood alongside the great fireplace, slabbed by a marble mantel, with iron candlesticks upon it. Reclining against the cushions of the settle was a large doll in a dress of red velvet – a Lucrezia Borgia doll, which wore a relentless smile and would have a key between its shoulder-blades so it could be wound up to walk. There in the lamplight it looked almost alive for a moment, as if it might move on its own, with a rustling of its Florentine skirts.

As Nick stared at the face of the doll it seemed to Della that all the blood seeped away from beneath the brown skin of his face and left him with a curiously drawn look.

It was as if the waxen-faced doll reminded him of a drowned child, and instantly Della swooped on the doll and tossed it out of sight into a dark corner of the room. 'I hate those things,' she said. 'They're neither childish nor adult – Nick, shall we go and start the stove for some coffee? I feel chilled!'

'Yes, let us revive ourselves with some coffee.' Very visibly he pulled himself out of that shocked trance created by the doll left on its own in this great echoing house, the discarded or forgotten playmate of a child who had probably preferred something more cuddly.

'This is the way to the kitchen,' said Nick, and they left the doll lying in the shadows, its mocking face to the wall.

CHAPTER NINE

THE kitchen of the villa was a vast one and it was a relief when the stove was lit, the kettle was bubbling, and there was a warm glow to dispel the feeling that until their advent the house ghosts had come alive in this place and had probably danced with that Borgia doll.

Nick was in the deep larder with the lamp, while Della spooned coffee from the caretaker's jar into the earthenware pot. There was only a pint-sized mug, so they would have to share that.

'Do you fancy some tinned spaghetti in tomato sauce?' Nick emerged from the larder with a can of the food in his hand, and a cobweb on his shoulder. 'It would seem that the owners of this place are going to sell, for holiday absentees would have left a little more in their cupboard, I should think, than a few cans of spaghetti and a box of stale rusks.'

'How shall we heat it?' Della automatically brushed the strands of web from his shoulder, and casual though the action was, her fingertips tingled as if she had trespassed . . . or more shockingly given him the idea that she wished to touch and be touched. She drew away from him and her fingers clenched at her side. When would she learn that she could not be casual with Nick, or behave as if she were here for the night with Joe Hartley!

'I shall stab a knife hole in the can and after we have made coffee we can place the can in the kettle and let it steam in the hot water.' A smile quirked the edge of his mouth, but his eyes were darkly intent behind the half lowered lashes, so that she knew him to be as tensed as she was, equally aware of every glance, every action, every nervous tremor.

'As a pair of Crusoes for the night we must make full use of our few resources.' He raised the lamp and examined the ceiling beams where hams, onions and peppers would have hung; then he played the light over the carved dresser with its rows of empty hooks. 'There is a sadness about houses unoccupied by a family, as mine in Tuscany is unoccupied except for a few servants. Strange to think, Della, that by this time tomorrow night I shall be there, and you will be in Greece awaiting the arrival of the *Gothic Star*–'

'I shan't.'

His black brows drew together as he stared at her, his shadow thrown high up the white wall so that Della seemed blended and lost in his darkness.

'I don't understand you,' he said, in a taut voice.

'I'm not flying on to Greece,' she said. 'I've decided to fly home to England.'

'I – see.' Nick turned away from her, releasing her from his towering shadow as he walked to the table and placed the lamp upon it. Then he went to the stove and lifted the kettle, wincing slightly at the heat of the handle. 'So you have decided that you cannot be away from your fiancé a day longer?'

'Yes,' she agreed, and it was a relief to have made up her mind, and faced the fact that she could not continue with a cruise which would be haunted for her by the memory of a man at the ship's rails, a coat thrown like a cloak around his shoulders while he raised a cigar to his lips and his dark head became shrouded in a mist of smoke. Only in England could she be safe from such a memory; shielded from it in the protective arms of Marsh.

Marsh loved her!

That was her only certainty and she had to get to him before the rumour reached him that she had had an affair with Nick Franquila.

There had been no affair, but a strange, poignant,

dangerous personage had crossed her path . . . and still it was night, and she was alone with him, and the dawn would not come for hours yet.

She gave a start as the coffee mug was pressed into her hand. 'Ladies first,' the drawl had returned to Nick's voice. 'It's strong and black and will encourage you.'

'Thank you.' She bent her head to the mug in order to avoid his eyes, and she drank her coffee while he busied himself with the can of spaghetti in tomato sauce. She gathered that they were going to eat it straight from the can, for there wasn't a dish or a plate on which to serve it.

'Why don't you sit down, *nina*?' He pointed to a wooden box that stood near the stove, and which the caretaker probably used as a makeshift seat.

'I might as well,' she agreed, but before taking it she refilled the mug with coffee and held it out to Nick, turned from the side from which she had drunk. 'Here you are, Nick, while it's still good and hot.'

'Grazie.' He took the mug and quite deliberately he turned it around in his hand and took a long, satisfying swig of the dark brew. Then he glanced up, right into her eyes, and she was glad the box was there so she could sit down. In that instant her knees had gone as weak as water, and though she told herself that it was reaction from the dramatic event of the *terremoto*, she knew what really caused that incredible wave of physical weakness.

Nick's lips had touched the place where hers had been, and it was as if she had felt that wilful underlip and that finely chiselled upper lip, taking possession of her mouth and imparting the pain and the passion that warred together in his lean body and his scarred soul.

'Well, we are not so bad here,' he said. 'We have good Italian coffee, a warm stove, and a supper of spaghetti to enjoy. Things could have been very much worse.'

'Yes,' she agreed, but she noticed that he had used quite a lot of the wood in order to get the stove going and what was left couldn't possibly last through the night. 'How shall we eat our spaghetti? With our fingers?'

'Too slippery.' He finished his coffee, took the lamp and returned to the larder for a moment. He emerged with the box of stale rusks. 'We can't eat these, but we can use a couple as spoons. Is that not good thinking?'

'Brilliant, Nick.' She broke into a slight smile, and encircling her knees with her arms she leaned towards the stove and enjoyed the warmth while they had it. 'For a member of the Latin *nobiltà* you are very resourceful if a trifle extravagant.'

'Extravagant.' He quirked an inquiring eyebrow. 'You made the coffee with a lavish hand.'

'And you made the fire. Most of the wood has burned away and from the feel of the draught from under that door, this house must be like a Frigidaire when night closes in and the fire goes out.'

'True, but we can burn that box you are sitting on, and perhaps find one or two other items to keep the fire going.' His smile became whimsical. 'I shall try to keep you warm and comfortable, Miss Friday.'

'That doll, in the hall, it's partly made of wax and should make a nice flare—'

'No!' His smile vanished and his eyes had a dark glitter to them. 'It has belonged to a child and I – I couldn't possibly burn it. The things a child has played with have almost a human quality – you would not know, but one day this man, this Marsh, he will put a baby in your arms—'

Nick broke off and turned to the stove, where she heard him mutter a curse as the handle of the kettle again scorched his hand as he lifted it from the stove. Della sat tense, staring at the tongues of flame as they writhed behind the bars ... it would be impossible for him to watch the burning of the doll, and yet a clean, harsh burning away of his bitter memories might act like the cauterizing of a wound, healing it, perhaps, for ever.

He washed the mug with some of the hot water, and said in rather a cool voice, 'Lucky for us the caretaker left water in the kettle – he probably brings his own, for the water supply is turned off at the main somewhere in the cellar, I expect. Do you mind sharing supper from the mug? It's all we have.'

'Of course I don't mind.'

'One cannot always tell with a cool Englishwoman what she minds and does not mind.' The point of his knife flashed downwards and Della saw the strong cutting motion of his wrist as he took the top off the can, lifting the circle of tin with the top of the knife and releasing the tasty aroma of the hot spaghetti and sauce. He emptied the steaming contents of the can into the earthenware mug, and then he glanced at Della. 'Bring your seat to the table and we will dig into this before it gets cold. Some hot food inside us will make us feel more human.'

She did as he directed, and together, using the rusks as spoons, they dipped and twirled the saucy strings of spaghetti and managed to make a fair meal between them.

'Not bad, eh?' Nick wiped his lips with his handkerchief, and scrubbed at a splash of tomato sauce on his shirtfront. 'I must say, Della *mia*, that you are quite the good sport to be marooned with – listen, that disturbance of the earth has given way to rain.'

They listened together to the rustle of the rain on the courtyard stones, and she thought of the midsummer flowers that lay wild over the hills, drowned now in that downpouring rain. She thought of the olive trees sprouting black from the ground, their leaves like many pointing pieces of silver. And the dark flames of the cypresses quenched in all that water. Italy seemed so alive in the sun, and so bedraggled in the storm.

As she turned to face Nick and to speak her thoughts, she saw something in his face which held her immobile. She saw his eyes drowned in memories, as if long ago he had sat like this in the kitchen of his house in the hills of Tuscany, making a picnic at the kitchen table while it rained, with the small girl who had to fill the empty places of his heart because his wife was unable to do so.

His strange bride, whom he had married because it had been arranged so, as it very often was among the families of the Italian nobility. There had been no spontaneous spark of love between them; no driving desire to be together. One day the introduction, then the betrothal, and finally the Cathedral wedding and the life with her that must have been curiously empty of warmth.

Of whom – oh, God, of whom did the waxen-faced Borgia doll truly remind him? Of Donaleza, whose dark and unbalanced mind had gradually filled with resentment of the child he loved?

There was a hissing sound as rain came down the chimney of the stove, and Nick arose to open the top and to place more wood upon the falling embers. Now there were only a few sticks left in the basket, and Della shivered in cold anticipation of the night to come. What were they going to do about getting some rest? There was the old cushioned settle in the hall, but no rugs of any sort.

'Nick—?'

'Yes, I know what you are thinking,' he said. 'We must get some rest and there is only one resting place in this entire house. There is very little fuel left, and we are both about to share the discomfort of a cold, uncomfortable night for the first time in our lives. You might even be thinking that we would have been just as well off to have stayed in the car, but there you are wrong. Where there has occurred one landslide there can occur another, and now it is raining so hard the likelihood of more rock and earth sliding down, perhaps to engulf the car, is a very strong one. Also we have been able to renew ourselves with a warm supper, so we are not so badly off.'

'I'm not saying we are, Nick,' she protested. 'You always assume that you can read my mind—'

'Upon this occasion I think perhaps I can read it,' he broke in. 'I believe you would be less on edge and more ready to regard this as an adventure if you were alone, let us say, with the good Joe Hartley – ah, I see from the quick widening of your eyes that I have struck a nerve! Instead of the good Joe as your companion in distress you have Nick Franquila, and he has the bad and reckless reputation. My dear,' he took a step towards her and his eyes were glinting in his lean, dark, utterly Latin face, 'are you afraid that by morning you will no longer be the flawless creature which Marsh Graham has created for himself?'

'Don't, Nick!' She jumped to her feet and the box fell over, creating a sharp noise on the stone floor that made all her nerves feel as if they had been exposed . . . as Nick had exposed the fear which lay like a little curled snake in her mind. 'It seems always to be something for you to mock, that I have not followed the fashion in permissiveness – like that woman Camilla, who can hand over her child to relatives so she can play around. I – I despise the very thought of being cheap and shop-soiled – a creature handed from man to man like a vulgar picture from a pin-up magazine.'

Della was breathing quickly with emotion as she faced Nick, clutching at words for her shield and her weapon. 'I don't doubt that you would prefer to be sharing this night with someone like Camilla – if it is true that you prefer the tawdry people of this world.'

'Are you asking if I prefer you to Camilla?' His eyes had narrowed and the lamplight flickered over the strongly defined bonework of his face but could not penetrate the shadow in his chin-cleft. The subtle power and pain of his personality was so striking that Della wondered how she found the nerve to parry insults with him. She would surely find a safer refuge in tears and a show of feminine fragility, but like a proud little fool she fought him on her feet, chin tilted, and eyes as stormy as the rain-swept night.

'I think Camilla is a little too willing and you prefer the sport of the chase,' Della rejoined. 'Or you pretend to.'

'Pretend, *nina*?' His tone of voice was as dangerous as his face. 'That is a risky word to use to a man who has you so entirely at his mercy in a lonely, empty house. Who would hear you if you screamed?...certainly not this man in England, who has such binding principles that he has never been tempted to melt you down into a warm, yielding, desirable woman. No, he prefers his lady of snow, his shapely block of ice, his white and gold Galatea on her pedestal. And you? What at heart are you? A girl who wants never to experience the true joy of being a woman?'

'Whatever I want – whatever I look forward to has nothing to do with you, Nick. Nothing!' And suddenly, without warning, her eyes were heavy with tears and that awful feeling of weakness swept over her. She turned away from him and crushed her eyelids down over the foolish tears. She didn't hear him approach and she shook all through as his hand came down on her shoulder.

'I hope, *nina*, that you really love this man,' Nick said quietly. 'And I hope he loves you. There is nothing crueller on this earth than a marriage made to suit circumstances rather than the heart. I speak from bitter experience and if I am tonight a man from whom you turn as if from the devil himself, then blame it on my youthful folly in thinking that love can come with patience, even endurance. Love is either a flame in the heart, or a stone on the soul, and we make our own pyre of lost illusions and broken dreams when we flout the gods of love.'

Abruptly he swung her to face him and placing a hand under her chin he made her look at him with her wet and stormy eyes. 'Will you be marrying Marsh Graham because you love him? Or will you become his bride in payment of a debt of gratitude?'

'I love him – love him!' she cried out defiantly. 'In all the years I've known him he has never hurt me the way you have. He has never spoken to me the way you have. He has treated me always with kindness and I hope to marry him soon – very soon.'

'Then *che serà, serà*,' said Nick, and his fingertips felt as if they left their imprint in her upper arms as he released her and took up the lamp. 'Come, we are going to have to bed down in the hall and it seems useless to keep the fire going in here.'

Della heard him as if from a distance, and she bent like a dreamer to pick up his jacket which had dropped from her shoulders when he had taken hold of her. She shivered, for the kitchen was going very cold as the fire sank, and there was only one place where they might make themselves reasonably comfortable. He picked up the wooden box and she followed him from the kitchen and along the passage to the hall. Their shadows joined in the lamplight, but they were already many miles apart. *Che serà, serà*, he had said. The dice were flung, the cards were called, and what had been said could not be unsaid.

In breaking up the wooden box Nick made noise enough to wake the shadows, and he seemed to know all about these heavy, high-sided settles which adorned these old halls, for after throwing the cushions in a heap on the floor he opened the top of the settle and revealed the capacious, hollow interior.

'We had one at Nonna's *palazzo* when I was a child.' His voice, his face, his manner, all were as sardonic as Della first remembered them. 'Angelo and I often used it as a hiding place – it was our *fortezza*, our knightly resting place, our hideaway for questionable objects brought in from the garden – see!' He revealed that in this instance the interior of the settle had been used as a storing place for old newspapers and magazines. As he lifted out several of the newspapers, something ran dark and leggy across his grey sleeve, and Della turned away with a shudder she couldn't repress. Normally she was unafraid of spiders and shadows and the rattle of windows in the rain. But tonight . . . tonight she was on edge as a young cat in a strange house, and the man who shared with her the night and the house was as unpredictable as the Italian weather.

She had always believed the Italian climate to be as smooth as the oil from its olive trees, gay and exuberant with sunlight, and filled with song.

But Italy was more than a holiday land . . . it was a place where people lived and loved and suffered. It was Nick's country, and as she watched him balling paper and making a small fire in the immense grate, she hoped with all her heart that he would stay in Italy and make a new life for himself.

'There!' as the flames leapt. 'That should take the chill off the air for a while.'

He returned to the settle and took out an armful of magazines, then before closing down the heavy lid he went over to where Della had thrown the Borgia doll and he placed it inside the settle, out of sight. 'These books will help augment our fuel when the wood gives out,' he said. He replaced the cushions after giving each one a thump and a shake to remove some of the dust. 'Come, Della, make yourself comfortable and perhaps try to get some sleep.' He shot his cuff and took a glance at his wristwatch. 'The ship has now set sail and I would advise you to forget about those people who might gossip. They are not to know that we are together.'

'Camilla knew,' she reminded him.

'So?' He shrugged his shoulders and dusted his hands on the sides of the trousers which had been so impeccable when they had started out from the ship.

'She was a – friend of yours.' Della held her own hands to the warmth of the burning wood in the grate.

'Please not to hesitate before that word friend,' Nick said crisply. 'I had my reasons for being a friend of that rather brittle young woman. Admired and courted, as she wished to be, she was a little nicer to that honey-haired child, who will be better off with her grandfather in Italy. I understand that he is not Italian born but has made his home in my country for many years. Yes, Honey will be fine with him, and her mother can then set about finding the husband she needs.'

'So it was Honey?' Della half-turned her head to look at him, the swing of her honey-gold hair against the fine-pale line of her profile, glistening in the firelight.

'Did you believe that I wished to be trapped by a gold-digger?' he drawled, hands thrust into his trouser pockets as he stood there, a sardonic smile on his face. 'Yes, how sheltered you have been, Dolly Neve. It must be the first time in your life that you have met a man like me . . . ah, dear, how well I recall those first moments on the ship when you stood there in sophisticated mink and dropped your orchids to the deck. Had it been any other female but one with such large and rather lost eyes I should have thought the orchids a come-on, and much more imaginative than the usual dropped handkerchief. Do you know what I thought?'

'No – and don't tell me!'

'I think I must, for I don't wish to go out of your life

being thought of as quite the rake. I looked at you and I thought to myself, "How beautiful she is, and how I would love to scorch her wings if it was not so obvious that she is not long out of the chrysalis".' His smile became whimsical. 'I am truly amazed that I have been so angelic as to return you to your fiancé without a scorch-mark on your golden wings.'

'You seem very sure that I would allow my – my wings to be scorched by you.' Della tilted her head just a fraction more, so that her hair fell over her eyes and concealed their expression from him.

'There have been moments – *cielo*, I am not a boy, Della! And now I suggest that you come and rest instead of drooping there in the firelight.'

'And what are you going to do, Nick?' She rose to her feet, her moment of weakness conquered as she pushed back the hair from her brow. 'We must both get some rest and you can't lie on a cold, dirty floor.'

'It was not my intention.' His eyes held hers. 'Now you are not to get me wrong, child, for at this moment I am being the very sensible Crusoe who has charge of this affair – ah, apologies, affair is not quite the word! But what I mean to say is that we must share the settle and keep each other warm – it is necessary, Della, so don't you dare to look at me as if I have something other than your welfare on my mind. Now we will be reasonable about this, eh?'

'I – I don't appear to have a choice,' she said. 'You will get pretty cold in your shirtsleeves, and I should hate to selfishly hog the settle—'

'Then that is settled.' A smile flickered on his lips. 'Now I imagine there is a *gabinetto* somewhere above stairs, so I am going to light the way so that you can make yourself comfortable before we go to bed. Come!'

'That, *signore*, must be a favourite word of Latin males to their hen-pecked females!'

'You have the gender wrong,' he reproved her. 'The Latin male crows, he does not lay eggs.'

They explored the upper regions of the villa and found a bathroom. It was terribly dusty and fearfully cold, but Della couldn't help but appreciate the common sense of the Latin male, and the thoughtfulness, for Nick allowed her to take the lamp into the *gabinetto* while he waited on the landing in the total darkness. She could hear him whistling to himself, and she smiled that she had ever thought that he didn't care a fig about anyone but himself.

She emerged from the bathroom with the lamp and handed it to him. 'It's dark in there,' she said.

'It's dark out here – will you mind for just a few moments?'

'Heavens, no!'

He disappeared and the door closed, and Della hugged herself in the cloak of his jacket, feeling the silk lining against her skin. The darkness all around her was absolute, and when she heard a faint scuttling sound, her skin seemed to crawl against the silk. And she could hear the wind moaning around the tall chimneys of the house, and finding a way in through the window cracks. She was so utterly glad when Nick rejoined her that she could have flung herself at him. He seemed to sense this, for he put his arm around her as they made their way down the stairs to the glow of their smoky fire in the hall.

Now had come the moment, she knew. A feeling almost bride-like, for she knew she was about to sleep in Nick's arms, and she knew it would be for the one and only time, with no rapture, no regrets, and no repeat performance.

With an impersonal efficiency he made her lie with her shoulders against the high back of the settle and he arranged a cushion so that her feet, from which he removed her shoes, were enclosed in a pocket of warmth.

Another cushion was tucked beneath her head and he put his jacket around her with her arms in the sleeves.

'Like a strait-jacket,' she nervously smiled.

'One of us is going to need it,' he muttered, and he went to the fireplace, where he spent about ten minutes tearing up the magazines and twisting them into paper sticks to keep the fire going for as long as possible.

It also seemed to Della that he was waiting for her to drop off to sleep, but she was too tense, despite her weariness, and his every action and every movement had such an effect on her nerves that she just couldn't relax. Again like a bride she seemed to be awaiting her bridegroom, as fearful as she was expectant.

As the fire smoked and flamed, Nick came to her, carrying the lamp. 'We can let this stay alight for as long as the oil lasts,' he said. 'In the morning I can leave money so the caretaker can buy some more. Well, *nina*,' he stood over her, 'are you now feeling more restful?'

She nodded, for her throat was too dry for speech. She saw him take off his shoes, set down the lamp so the flickering light was not in their eyes, and her heart pounded as he slid on to the settle beside her and arranged his long body so she was protected and warmed by his legs and arms.

He spoke abruptly: 'Just think of yourself as a child,' he ordered. 'Pretend you are Honey.'

But it wasn't as easy as that. All she could think of, with his arms around her, here in this dim and smoky hall, was that no one would ever believe that she had slept, unkissed, in the arms of Nick Franquila. None but she would ever know that he could be so strangely kind, and as the warmth and drowsiness stole over her, she yielded to the forbidden joy of being close to him, and suddenly she slept as if, indeed, she were a child.

She awoke hours later as naturally as a child, her eyes

seeking the daylight that straggled through a grimy window. At first she was bemused and only conscious of physical warmth and well-being. From her toes to her throat she was bathed in that luscious warmth, and all around there was a stillness as dawn struggled out of the arms of night. There was no sound of rain . . . but beneath her ear there was a curious, regular pulsing . . . and her bemusement fled as she realized that her head was at rest upon the breast of the man in whose arms she was closely cradled. It was the most awesome sensation of her life . . . the most intimate thing which had ever happened to her.

She lay very still, as if the slightest movement, now, would wake him and rob her of the astounding discovery that even a man such as Nick was made vulnerable by sleep . . . he was a Samson shorn of all his power and assurance . . . his dark head thrown back against a worn silk cushion, his lips slackened into a semblance of youth . . . a youth which the darkness of his beard had to dispel.

Now it was morning she ought to wake him and pull out of his arms, but she was gripped by reluctance, for he was so profoundly asleep, and so lost to all the past, and all the future. He dreamed like a boy again, and she was loath to disturb him . . . not yet . . . not just yet . . and closing her eyes again she rested against the heart that she hoped his return to Tuscany would heal one day.

She seemed to slumber awhile between waking and dreaming, but it was no dream when her eyes opened again and she found Nick looking at her. It was a soundless, timeless, searching look, as if he were making a memory of her face, as she made a memory of his. Even ungroomed, she thought, he retained his rakish attraction. With his hair ruffled, his chin unshaven, and his eyes still slumbrous, he did not repel her. He was like a tiger, she told herself, roused in his den and ready to go hunting.

'Hungry?' he asked, and he was looking at her as if *she* roused his appetite.

At once she felt all the panic which had been absent while he slept. Now he was awake and aware as she was of how closely they had come together in the night, so that she seemed tucked within the long, hard curve of his body, shackled by his legs and his arms. He was no longer the vulnerable sleeper, and she could feel the muscles of his arms as he held her, the vital aliveness of his skin against hers.

'Breakfast would be welcome,' she said primly. 'But I don't much fancy spaghetti out of a can.'

'Nor I.' He looked at her a moment longer, and then rasped a hand over his chin. '*Cielo*, no wonder you are studying me like a bird hypnotized by a big cat! I must look all fur and prickles to a girl who has never before slept with a man.'

'I – I didn't exactly do that,' she protested. 'You said to keep warm – we had to share this couch.'

'All the same,' he quirked a wicked black eyebrow, 'it is a new experience for you, seeing how shaggy the male of the species looks first thing in the morning.'

'But no new experience for you,' she flashed back, 'seeing how a woman looks!'

'Naughty, naughty,' he mocked, and again his eyes roved lazily over her ruffled hair. 'I have never yet seen how guilty an entirely innocent woman can look when she wakes up to find herself in a man's arms. All you are longing for is to be out of my arms, eh?'

'If you don't mind, Nick.' Her gaze dropped to his throat, with the chain of his medal drawn across the brown skin like a golden scar. 'We have that long drive to Naples and I – I have so much to do. My flight home to book, and a travelling dress to buy. This one I'm wearing must look a wreck!'

'Yes, as you say there is much to do.' Abruptly his arms

fell away from her and he removed himself from the settle in a lithe, unwinding movement of his long body. He stretched his arms and loosened his muscles, and then gave Della a helping hand.

Once upon her feet she and Nick surveyed each other and had to laugh. 'We both look wrecks,' she said.

'Indeed we do, and there is little we can do about it. We have no fire to boil the water remaining in the kettle, but I suppose we can give our faces a handkerchief scrub. After which I suggest we make our way to the car and turn back in the direction of Amalfi. We can breakfast there and take the train to Naples. It will in the long run be quicker that way.'

Nick had it all organized in his mind, so Della fell in with his orders. Half an hour later they crossed the overgrown courtyard of the villa which had sheltered them for the night; the sun was now splashing its brightness over the damp stones and the trees that still emitted the smell of rain. Webs glittered among the shrubs, and birds swooped on the fallen leaves where insects lay trapped and made their gaily derisive morning noises.

At the gates of the villa Della and Nick glanced back in unison; in daylight it looked empty and pathetic, with most of the upper windows shuttered.

'Not *arrivederci* but good-bye,' Nick murmured, and Della had the rather sad feeling that he was already saying good-bye to her.

They made their way down the slope of the road, which was still very quiet except for the birds. They didn't speak very much, and found the coupé awaiting them where they had left it last night. A lot of the fallen earth had puddled into mud and Della was about to walk through it to the side of the car when Nick stopped her and without saying a word swept her up in his arms. He carried her to the car and lowered her to her feet beside it. He unlocked the doors after she handed him the keys from her purse – put there for safe-keeping. Then they were inside the car and he was carefully backing it along the road until they reached a bend and he was able to make the turn that would lead them back to Amalfi.

There, as he had promised, they had a much needed breakfast, with plenty of coffee, thick slices of ham, and eggs done to a turn by the plump, jolly cook of the same *trattoria* where they had lunched the day before. Nick made inquiries about trains and by noon they were aboard the one bound for Naples.

Della dozed with her head against the prickly plush, and all the way to Naples the wheels of the train seemed to rattle out a message of farewell to Italy and to Nick. Behind her closed eyelids Della felt the burning sensation of tears, for each rushing mile was bringing her nearer and nearer to the moment when she would hold out her hand and say farewell to Nick.

'Forever, and forever, farewell—
    If we do meet again, why, we shall smile.'

Upon their arrival in Naples, Nick booked her in at the Vittorio Hotel, as if already it would be wiser for them not to be together at his hotel for these few remaining hours. He then asked the desk clerk to arrange for her a booking on the earliest flight to London. The clerk rang the airport and then reported that there would be a seat on the night flight to London Airport, if that would be suitable.

'Nothing earlier?' she asked urgently, while Nick stood beside her and looked quite impassive, as if all that mattered now was that her arrangements for departure be settled.

The clerk inquired again, and then shook his head.

'Then the night flight will have to do,' she said. 'Please book it for me.'

'Si, signorina.'

Nick drew her away from the desk and they stood beside a potted palm while he said that he now had to go to his own hotel to bathe and change and collect his luggage, delivered there the day before from the *Gothic Star.*

'I can return to say good-bye, if you wish?' he said.

But Della bravely shook her head. 'Let's get it over with, Nick,' she replied, and this was the moment when she held out her hand for their good-bye handshake. But he didn't take her hand. He suddenly inclined his head with Latin formality. 'You have my best wishes, Della,' he said. 'May you be happy.'

And then he was gone, striding out through the swing doors, and leaving such an empty space that Della almost screamed out a protest. She stood there by the potted palm for what seemed a million shattered moments, and then she pulled herself together. Clenching her fingers around her purse, she went out on to the Corso Uberto and sought the shops where she might buy new lingerie and a dress, not to mention toiletries, including a packet of pine-seeds for a bath that would help soothe away the ache which had spread from her heart to every other portion of her body.

Carrying her purchases in a holdall she returned to the Vittorio Hotel and applied for the key to her room. Once there she locked herself in and stripped off her creased dress . . . the dress which yesterday had looked so cool and fresh.

For about an hour she soaked in warm, bubbly water, and she tried with all her will to shut from her mind that very last glimpse she had had of Nick's face. He had looked so – so formal, so withdrawn, as if they had not really shared those hours that she must stretch through all the nights to come . . . those hours marooned together in the hills beyond Sorrento, cut off by a landslide.

With a shiver of distress she could not control she stepped from the bath and enfolded herself in a large towel. Then she walked through to the bedroom and taking up the telephone asked that a pot of tea be sent to her room. Oh God, how she needed a cup of tea! How she needed the semblance of courage that it would give her!

She dressed in the new lingerie, and the almond-green linen dress which she had bought off the peg in one of the really good Italian shops on the Corso. She brushed her hair until it shone, and made up her face in her usual light-handed way, and was feeling a little more composed when the waiter arrived with her tray of tea and biscuits. Also on the tray were her flight tickets, which had been sent to the hotel by messenger. She thanked the waiter and tipped him, and then settled down to pass the remainder of the afternoon in the seclusion of her room.

Darkness was drifting in, and the many lights of the Corso were gradually coming to life, like night flowers, when all at once the telephone rang on the table beside the bed and Della almost jumped out of her skin, for so unexpected was the sound. She stared from the window at the faint pale outline of the telephone, and she thought of Nick. Was he ringing her to underline their good-bye? Oh, but surely Nick would be gone from Naples by now, on his way to Tuscany, going back to the life he had left all those years ago.

She approached the telephone and lifted the mouthpiece, feeling at the same time the shakiness of her legs as she stood there and spoke her name at the caller.

'Della?'

Her heart jolted. 'Marsh?' But it couldn't be! How would he know where to reach her? 'Is it really you, Marsh?'

'Who else would it be?' His voice came with unexpected harshness along the line, which faintly crackled to let her know that he was calling from a distance . . . from

England. 'Were you expecting a call from your Italian lover?'

Lover? She stared at the telephone as if it could bite her . . . and indeed it was biting her, for never had she heard Marsh speak in such a way to her. 'Marsh, what are you talking about?'

'I'm sure you know,' his words whipped back at her. 'Last night I had a ship-to-shore phone call from the *Gothic Star*, and I was informed that you had left the ship in order to spend time in Italy with this Italian *conte*. I shall take your word for it if you tell me it isn't true – if you can give me a proper explanation as to why you missed the boat, and why you're still in Naples.'

'Marsh,' her voice shook, 'how did you contact me here at the hotel?'

'Because I was informed last night of where this *conte* would be staying. Are you staying with him, Della? Is he there in the room with you, listening while I demand an explanation of your behaviour?'

'Demand . . . explain . . . always behave as you see fit!' Suddenly her blue-green eyes were blazing in the darkness of the room, shot through by the neons of the Corso theatres and restaurants. 'If I say I'm all alone are you going to believe me, Marsh? Or if I say that last night I was cut off by a landslide and couldn't get back to the ship, are you going to accept my word as the truth?'

'Cut off?' he cut in. 'With this Italian *conte*?'

'Don't keep referring to Nick in that way!' Anger with Marsh stirred through her, and all the years of restriction, of being grateful, of being fond of someone and making believe it felt like love, came storming to the surface of Della's personality. 'All last night I was with Nick . . . he kept me in good spirits, made me warm in his arms . . . brought me alive. Alive, Marsh, so that I want to be a woman, not a waxen doll who sings when the strings are pulled, who smiles politely at all the right people, at the right moments. Marsh, did you ever want a girl called Dolly, with windblown hair, smudged lipstick, and a run in her nylons? Did you ever really want a wife? Tell me now, and if it's true that you can love an imperfect creature who has rather got herself talked about with another man, then I'll believe you and come home to you.'

After she had said this, there was a prolonged silence at the other end of the line, and then at last he spoke, this man who had always been kind, but more generous with his money than with his emotions.

'What do you mean, Della?' he asked. 'When you say you spent all last night with this Italian fellow?'

And knowing she would shatter the porcelain image which he had of her, Della told him the truth. 'I slept with Nick Franquila, and he behaved like a perfect gentleman.'

This time there was a shorter silence. 'I don't believe you, Della – the fellow is a rake, not a gentleman.' And then the line clicked dead against Della's eardrum, and she knew that for Marsh she was an item in his collection which had suddenly lost its value and had no more place in that perfect, speckless house of his on Richmond Hill. He had taught her truth and when she told it, he thought she told a lie. The only real, rough, ravishing truth was that she loved Nick . . . Nick who had asked if she wished to become part of a collection instead of being loved for herself . . . herself . . . Dolly Neve.

She would still leave Italy, for it was still too poignantly remindful of Nick. She would return to England and seek to make a singing career apart from Marsh. She would find a way to be happy . . . and she would pray that Nick also found some happiness at last and did not rejoin that gay carnival that led nowhere.

She packed into the holdall the clothing she had discarded, shrugged herself into the doeskin jacket she had bought, and prepared to leave for the airport. She briefly rang the desk to say that she would be leaving and would they make up her bill, then she quietly let herself out of the room and locked the door.

This was the hour when there was a lull between guests hurrying down for dinner, or a night out on the town, and Della rode down in the lift all alone. She stepped out and there was the marble reception desk just across the expanse of red carpet. There was the potted palm where she had said good-bye to Nick ... there the cane chair ... there the long legs, impeccably clad in dark grey suiting, a lean hand hung down at the side of them, a crested ring on the small finger, a cigar locked between the long fingers and slowly raised, until a cloud of aromatic smoke drifted from the palm-concealed lips.

She had to be dreaming, of course. Nick was miles away by now, and this was just a guest at the hotel, lounging there with a cigar before going in to dinner ... or perhaps he waited to take a lady dancing?

Her legs felt as if the bones were melting, yet she had to walk past the potted palm on her way to the desk, she had to make those few yards somehow, and see a stranger's eyes brush her face, and see a stranger who only bore the semblance of a noble ghost.

Her fingers tightened on the holdall and she willed her legs to carry her to the desk. She wouldn't look ... and then she just had to look ... and with a rakish, and wholly possessive smile, Nick rose from the depths of the cane chair and came towards her with his illimitable dark grace. No guest ... no ghost ... but a very vital human being, who when he reached her side quickly slid around her body a warm, supporting arm.

'Let us settle your bill and be off,' he said, almost casually. 'You will be travelling by night, *mia cara,* but on a train, not a plane, and not to London but to Tuscany.'

In a sort of daze she left the hotel with him, and there at the kerb was a taxi piled with luggage. They entered the taxi and it set off along the busy Corso, heading for the railway station and not the airport.

'Nick—' She was in his arms now, and his eyes were laughing at her in the lights that streamed past the taxi windows. 'You must explain or I shall go crazy.'

'Being in love is being a little crazy,' he smiled. 'A call – long-distance – came through to my hotel. It was, to put it bluntly, your fiancé assuming that you were there with me. I had to arrange for the call to be transferred to you at the Vittorio, and at the same time I knew I could not leave Naples until I saw you again, after you had taken that call. I waited in the lounge of the Vittorio, and I told myself that if I saw a girl with a happy face I would leave and keep to myself what that girl had done to my heart, and all those feelings I felt sure were dead in me, and which she kindled into warm fire again with her lovely face, and virtue, and voice. But when I saw you, when I arose from that seat beside the palm-tree, I knew you might faint if I did not quickly take hold of you. And when I took hold of you, I knew you were mine and that no more did this man in England stand between us. And now I will go a little crazy if you don't tell me, Dolly, what you said to him?'

'Why, Nick,' she touched his lean, dark face with her hand, 'I told him the truth, for he asked for that. I told him that all last night I was with you, and he chose not to believe that a man could be so perfectly the gentleman.'

'I will tell you something else, my lady.' And in her ear Nick softly whistled *Tio amo*. 'You seemed surprised that I should know the song so well, but you see, I wrote it.'

'Nick—' she looked astounded, 'you are that mysterious Italian composer? You wrote *Giovanni, Amore*?'

'Yes – think how talented will be our children.' And then the smile in his eyes gave way to a raw blaze of love, and his lips on hers were telling her that she was part of him, born for him, never to part from him. '*Madonnina, amore*,' he whispered.